COSCOM
ENTERTAINMENT

ALSO BY A.P. FUCHS

Blood of My World Trilogy

Discovery of Death
Memories of Death
Life of Death

Undead World Trilogy

Blood of the Dead
Possession of the Dead

THE AXIOM-MAN™ SAGA
(listed in reading order)

Axiom-man
Episode No. 0: First Night Out
Doorway of Darkness
Episode No. 1: The Dead Land
City of Ruin
Of Magic and Men (comic book)

OTHER FICTION

A Stranger Dead
A Red Dark Night
April (writing as Peter Fox)
Magic Man (deluxe chapbook)
The Way of the Fog (The Ark of Light Vol. 1)
Devil's Playground (written with Keith Gouveia)
On Hell's Wings (written with Keith Gouveia)
Zombie Fight Night: Battles of the Dead
Magic Man Plus 15 Tales of Terror
Undeniable

ANTHOLOGIES (as editor)

Dead Science
Elements of the Fantastic
Vicious Verses and Reanimated Rhymes: Zany
Zombie Poetry for the Undead Head

NON-FICTION

Book Marketing for the
Financially-challenged Author

POETRY

The Hand I've Been Dealt
Haunted Melodies and Other Dark Poems
Still About A Girl

Go to
www.canisterx.com
&
www.undeadworldtrilogy.com

BLOOD OF MY WORLD

Discovery of Death

A. P. Fuchs

COSCOM ENTERTAINMENT
WINNIPEG

ISBN 978-1-926712-81-9

PUBLISHED BY COSCOM ENTERTAINMENT
www.coscomentertainment.com
Text set in Garamond; Printed and bound in the USA
COVER ART BY C.J. HUTCHINSON

For Buttons

Discovery of Death

Kissing Rose was like kissing blood: warm, smooth, sweet; a gentleness to her lips that made Zach cry out for more. When their lips met, his heart held hers and she his; her life flashed before his eyes and he knew her better than she knew herself.

As their lips playfully melded, separated, merged, he held her close, his embrace gentle and careful, yet firm enough so she knew he'd never let go. Her arms wrapped tightly around his neck, he sensed that if it was possible, she'd pull him deep into herself and make their bodies one. Instead, Rose's hands tugged behind his neck, her fingers stroking its nape, letting him know how much she loved him.

Tongues gliding across each other's, Zach was ever cautious that Rose didn't accidentally drag her tongue across his fangs and cut herself. The last thing he wanted to do was hurt her. They'd already been down the road of pain, loneliness and separation. For something to happen to set them on that path again, he couldn't bear it.

Even now, standing here with her, holding her, kissing her, there was the underlying trepidation that something might go wrong.

Zach's heart raced with phantom beats, his uneasiness at the prospect of losing her distracting him from their kiss.

Rose must have sensed it because she pulled slightly away and said, "What's wrong?"

"I just . . . I love you so much," he whispered. "I never thought—"

She placed the soft skin of her fingertips across his lips. "Shhh." And drew her to him.

Their lips met and Zach's world exploded in flashes of Rose growing up, a little girl with brown hair in pigtails wrapped in purple ribbon all the way to the gorgeous sixteen-year-old she was now.

The images—flying photographs wrapped in light—not just mere pictures but each a snapshot of Rose's time on this earth oozing with meaning and life, their display not just impacting his mind's eye but also his heart. Though each image flashed but for an instant, the sensations crashing through him drew on, the events depicted happening in real time. A nightmare when she was three; a pizza party for her and her girlfriends when she was six; the cake falling off its tray as her mother tried to bring it to her on her tenth birthday; her first pimple; her dad giving her the keys to the car when she got her license.

It was Rose's life that kept Zach connected to the realm of the living. His life . . . he didn't know it, at least not in the way he should. These past few weeks with Rose were all he knew by way of life.

It was a few months ago that he emerged from the dark, unsure of who he was and how he wound up in a crypt in Eagle Park Cemetery.

It was several months since he became a vampire.

What We Created

Always remember
Do not forget
The world we created
Together

I'm at its edge now
My feet on the line
Gazing off
Hoping to see you

Instead it's just me
The line
And a chamber of nothing
Before me

Without you
I can't see
Without you
I can't breathe

You are my five senses
Six
If you count my heart
Seven, my soul

Always remember
Do not forget
The life we created
Together

1

Rebirth . . .

THE DUSTY TEXTURE of nylon rubbed against his fingertips. At first it was difficult to see, but as his eyes adjusted, all was bathed in a gray hue as if moonlight was the source of light here in this dim place. Only a scant few inches away, bluish-gray waves of fabric were before his eyes. The musty scent of age and antique doilies greeted his nostrils with such potency he thought he was going to sneeze. But he didn't. Instead, his senses absorbed the crisp smell and he was at ease with its strength.

A part of him was comfortable here in this plush chamber. He was pressed in from all sides by pillowy fabric and padding. It was a narrow place, probably no more than the length of his body.

I don't really know. His inner voice seemed louder, clearer than it was supposed to be. Yet at the same time he felt at home here and a part of him wished to sleep, because something inside said it was not yet time to wake and emerge from this place.

Worms slithering in soil somewhere beyond caught the attention of his ears and he squirmed inside his plush cocoon, thinking these things were somewhere in here with him. He glanced side to side and didn't see anything.

Leaves rustled on trees and he instinctively drew his hand to his face within the confines of this tight space when he heard a leaf break free of its branch and flutter through the air down toward his face. But nothing touched his skin.

Footsteps thumped from somewhere above, slightly muted, like someone walking on carpet. Wait, not someone. More than one. At least five. Yes, five people. Ten separate feet.

For a second he thought they were going to step on him, their feet bursting through the fabric in front of his face and squish him. But they didn't.

"I can't stay here," he whispered. There was a need to properly address himself but he couldn't remember what that address might be. A title? A name? A combination of both? All he knew was he lay here alone with vibrant activity above him.

He placed both palms against the fabric, his fingertips once more discovering its smooth *under*-texture in a powdery coating, and behind that, wads of cotton, and behind that still—oak.

He pushed. At first, it seemed that the hard oak on the other side of the padded fabric would not move, but a moment later, its heavy weight gave way and pushing it aside was as easy as throwing off a blanket. The wood moved up and over to the side like a lid, its hinges stopping it before it completely fell off to the left side. Musty air washed over him and a dark ceiling made up of rock and dirt hung overhead. A second lid—black, scratched and old—still covered his legs. He sat up, reached forward and lifted that one as well.

He sat there and recognized what he had been inside: a coffin. He looked around. Other coffins lined the floor along with his in a square, each inset in the walls made of black rock, some coated in mud, others not. One coffin sat in the middle of the room.

His insides split in two: one half wanted to run screaming and get away from this place; the other sensed its warmth, an atmosphere of home. It was wrong. It was right.

Fatigue rushed over him and he laid back down and closed his eyes. Immediately, discomfort set in and he sat up and hopped out of the coffin.

The others all around him were still closed. Were there people inside there, too?

Are they dead? I'm not. Sleeping? Seems right. "Wait. No. Not right. Maybe. Sleeping." It was difficult to think straight.

The footsteps above returned and he wanted to see if perhaps whomever they belonged to could help him. Using the footsteps as a guide, he listened as they traveled over the rocky ceiling and followed their sound out of the cave and into a shallow-staired tunnel. The stairs led up and the footsteps slowly transformed from coming from above him to coming from parallel to him, when he finally reached the top of the stairwell to a stone door.

Unable to see a handle, he placed his palms on the jagged stone, trying to find something to use as one. There was none. Leaning into it, he focused his weight on his palms, pressed, and tried sliding the door. It moved to the side and revealed a small room no bigger than a closet, the walls on either side composed of marble-encased coffins, inset in shallow marble shelves.

Not bothering to read the writing above the graves, he headed straight for the main door. This one was iron and had a handle. He pressed down on it. After a loud clunk, the door unlatched and opened.

Fading sunlight streamed in and his hands immediately burst in flames.

"Ahhhh," he yelled and buried his hands beneath his

armpits, extinguishing them. Part of the light touched his toes, but didn't seem to bother them through his running shoes.

He checked his hands. Deep red blotches dotted his skin, some as large as coins, others mere pinpricks. Hands shaking, the pain from the burns began to dissipate and the blotches on his skin began to shrink then altogether disappear.

"Whoa . . ." he said despite instinctively knowing there was nothing special about what he saw.

Carefully, he reached for the handle and again the fading sunlight licked his skin and sent a stream of fire across it. With a yelp, he shook his hand off, getting rid of the flame.

He looked himself over. He wore a jean jacket, white T-shirt and blue jeans. He slid his hand in the cuff of his jacket, covering it, then used the covered hand to reach forward and close the door. When it closed, he sat on the floor, not wanting to go back downstairs, but also unable to go outside.

Sun. It was more an image in his mind than a word—yellow, spherical, fiery—and the image brought a foreboding sense of danger. Why the notion was coming to him now and not before, he didn't know, but it also provided an epiphany: the sun was dangerous.

Moon. Another image, the white, bright and perfect sphere of space rock in the sky. Safety. Protection. Freedom.

He would wait until the moon came.

"It comes at night," he said, assuring himself there was a time set aside for him to go outside and get help.

Sitting there, legs drawn up to his chest, focusing was difficult. His head was full, but he had a hard time deciphering what that *fullness* was. It was like waking up with brain fog and time was needed to start seeing clearly.

Somewhere in that jumble was the answer to why he was here. He obviously knew what certain things were: coffins, sun, moon, shoes, jacket. But there was more there that he couldn't quite tap into just yet. A name was one of them. He knew what a name was, but didn't know what *his* name was. At the same time, he knew the significance of a name and the history and identity it brought. Without one . . . he was free and unfettered by having nothing attached to himself, but he was also lost and without an anchor to help give him purpose.

A name was more than just a word. A name was the connecting point of all facets of life: soul, past, present, future. Actions, words, feelings. Thoughts, abilities, desires.

He needed a name.

He needed it to be dark.

Z

Ever since Zach Mohansen went missing, Rose Jordan didn't give too much thought to her appearance anymore. She remembered what it was like a few months ago—back when Zach was still around—how she'd be sure to take a shower every morning before school, curl her long brown hair into loose ringlets, and apply just enough makeup to highlight her lips and bright hazel eyes. Every outfit was selected with care, usually something white, as Zach once said that every time he saw her wearing white she reminded him of an angel.

There was so much excitement in those days. She'd barely have the desire to eat breakfast, her heart beating with such eagerness to see him that it chased her appetite away. She remembered her friend, Stephanie, once telling her that it's usually the first three or four months of a relationship that was—as she put it—"hot and heavy," the thrill of being with someone you really liked always new, something you never quite got used to.

It was like that with Zach. That boy seemed to appear out of thin air. Not literally, of course, as he'd gone to school with her since as far back as she could remember, but she never gave him much thought. He didn't have many friends, and those he did have weren't what she'd call popular or even cool. They seemed to be the kind of guys that were friends simply because there wasn't anyone else to be friends with. Whatever works, she supposed, but she knew it was that kind of shallowness that had kept her from him for so long.

Zach was special, a kind of hidden astonishment. Growing up, he was tall and gangly, with too much brown hair in a mess of waves atop his head, and acne that made one cringe at first glance. It was the summer before tenth grade that everything changed. Zach went home at the end of the school year like everyone else. He didn't even attend the junior high prom. Rose thought she overheard somewhere he'd been sick, though she suspected he never really felt like he would fit in and so avoided the party altogether.

But it was that summer that changed everything.

Zach came to school on the first day after the break, and Rose, who had been searching the halls for her first class, stopped in her tracks when she saw him. He hadn't looked her way. He didn't have to. Something about him gripped her. At the time, she didn't know who he was. He stood there in the hallway, a small white slip of paper in one hand, a stack of books in the other, his eyes glued to the piece of paper. It was like fireworks went off in her chest and she was immediately captivated by this guy with the cute brown locks that sat in a loose tussle on his head, a clear complexion, and a slender but muscular build beneath his black T-shirt and blue jeans. It was only upon further inspection did she realize who he was. Immediately, her cheeks flushed and she forced herself to look away and continue searching for her class. When she passed him in the hallway, she couldn't help but look up and steal another glance. Zach looked her way, gave her a soft smile, and continued on.

Rose had stopped in her tracks again, unable to fully wrap her head around why she was drawn to him.

He wasn't the boy she once knew anymore.

◆ ◆ ◆

Rose came down the stairs for breakfast, her heart aching. Getting over Zach's vanishing act was something she was still trying to deal with.

Her father sat at the table, scanning the newspaper, his dark eyes even more prominent these days thanks to his graying hair that seemed to take on another hint of silver every morning.

"Morning, pumpkin," he said, and flipped the page.

"Hi," she said softly and sat down across from him, wondering when he would stop calling her that silly pet name. Not only was it uncool, but she found it demeaning. A constant reminder of how he refused to see the woman she was growing up to be.

If the Jordan household was known for anything, it was routine. Her bowl and spoon were already set before her on the table, the box of cereal to her right, the milk to her left.

She glanced to the empty seat near the window. Zach had sat there the few times he had come for dinner. She could still see him sitting there now, a ghost of good times past.

Her father bent down the top half of the newspaper and gazed past it. "Better hurry. Don't want to be late."

"Yeah," she said and stood up.

"Not going to eat?"

"Not very hungry this morning."

"Got to have something. Breakfast is the most important meal of the day and all that."

She nodded. "Where's Mom?"

"Had an early showing. I'm catching up with her shortly after some paperwork."

"You guys are going to be busy today, right?" she asked. It was a rhetorical question. Her parents owned their own real estate business and were busy every day. Weekends were optional the same way relaxing evenings were.

"Got to meet some people around five. Depends how it goes. Hope to be home just after six."

Rose went to the fridge and pulled out the lunch she had made the night before. As she went past her father to the door beyond, she noticed a cut along his jawline.

"You okay?" she asked.

"Hm?" He bent the paper down again.

"You got—" She ran her index finger along the side of her jaw.

"Oh, that," he said and put a hand over it. "It's nothing. Cut myself something fierce shaving."

"You might want to put a band-aid on it. Looks pretty deep."

He pulled his hand away and checked his palm. "It's not bleeding; I should be all right." He set the paper down with his other hand. "Sure you don't want anything? You need to eat, Rose."

"I know."

Her dad's eyes slightly glazed over. He already knew why she wasn't hungry. They'd already talked about it. All he told her was, "You got to hang in there. Things will be fine in the end. Boys come and go."

The words never gave her comfort, and the last comment infuriated her, but she knew he meant well.

"See you later," she said.

"Have a good day."

"You, too."

Rose headed out the door and walked slowly to the bus stop.

R

Red flower petals floated past his vision and despite the darkness of the crypt, they were as vivid as bolts of lightning across a black sky. There was meaning in flowers, he knew, though the knowledge of such was more an *impression* than actual fact.

Tired, the young man's eyes aching for sleep, he wasn't sure if sleep would even come. Not here. Not like this. He was back downstairs. Despite the gloom of the underground tomb feeling like home, a part of him recognized this wasn't a place for sleep, at least not the kind that was temporary.

He stood, and instinctively raised his arms to stretch. Instead, his muscles didn't budge as they were already loose and teeming with life.

The dark took on a new shape, one where each shadow grew darker, black as pitch, the surrounding areas growing to a rich gray. Suddenly, all became clear and he could see his surroundings perfectly.

The coffin across from him was made of stone, rich and ornate carvings decorating its lid and sides. They were pictures of men and women in robes, all with long flowing hair, each person entangled in passionate embraces. However, where he expected their lips to meet in a kiss, instead the heads were nestled in the crook of the other's neck, as if seeking intimacy there instead.

He drew close to the coffin and touched its lid. Its stone should be cold, he felt, but was instead luke warm to the touch, borderline *without* any temperature at all.

Other coffins lined the room, one on each side along with the one in the middle: five total. All were as beautiful as the one before him, all bearing similar markings as the one he had his fingers upon now.

He pulled his hand away and started to walk around the coffin in the center of the room, searching for a name.

There was none.

He took a deep breath and looked at his hands. They stood out bright and gray against the monochrome of his vision.

"I am dead," he said, though not of his own will. It was more a blurting out of a thought than anything else.

The coffin lid in front of him moved, stone grinding on stone as it slid along the box it covered.

"Dead, but very much alive," a female voice said from within the wooden box inside.

The lid continued to move of its own accord, as if automated, until it slid completely to one side and lowered itself to the ground, light as a feather.

The young man stumbled back a step, his muscles bursting with even more energy than they were before.

From inside the inky blackness of the coffin, dark and partly rotted wooden lids flipped open. A female arose, standing straight up and away from him. She wore a long, form-fitting black dress with lace around the cuffs of her sleeves. Her long, smooth black hair hung past her backside. When she glanced at him over her shoulder, she offered a sweet smile with bright red lips.

She turned on the spot without shuffling her feet, and brought her hands up across her breast in an X.

"Welcome home, my son," she said.

The young man's mind froze and falling red petals rained in front of his vision once again.

In an instant, the woman was in front of him. "Do not be frightened. Mommy's here." She glanced up, then met his eyes again. "Oh, how I've waited for this day. We had to wait until you were ready, you see. We had to wait until—" She stopped speaking, probably catching his wide-eyed questioning gaze. "Are you frightened?"

Oddly enough, he wasn't. He knew his heart should be thundering in his chest, but instead there was . . . nothing . . . only this sense of confusion, jumbled thoughts and incoherent questions.

But he nodded anyway.

"Now, now," she said, "don't lie to your mother."

"My mother?"

"Oh Zach, I'm sorry. You obviously took the change hard."

He wanted to speak, to ask what she was talking about, but the words wouldn't form.

"This happened to your brother as well," the woman said. A moment later, she appeared on the other side of the coffin, as if intentionally giving him some distance. "Some retain their memory of life once transformed, others don't. Rather, we all do in the end, but sometimes not right away. It seems you don't remember anything, do you?"

"I-I woke up . . . in the dark. I got out of the, um, coffin and went outside. But" —the searing memory and phantom pains of catching on fire forced him to clench his fists— "but . . . the heat. So hot."

"The sun," she said. "You cannot live in the sun any longer."

"I don't understand."

"You will, in time." She appeared right in front of him again. Her speed—how did she do that? It was only now he really took notice. This woman could do things that—His vision went dark for a moment, then when it cleared, he found himself laying on the floor, the woman at his side.

"You need to rest, Zach," she said.

Zach? "Who's—"

"You are."

"Zach?"

She nodded. "Mommy will make everything all right."

G

Rose endured the school day like any other, wandering from class to class until finally the bell rang at three.

The walk to the bus stop took incredibly long, each step strained with the phantom sensations of Zach's hand in hers, the two spending as much time together as possible—even on the bus—until they'd get off at separate stops.

She knew she wasn't supposed to feel this way, at least in terms of missing him so much.

There was puppy love and then there was the real thing. Her father always told her that until you were an adult, puppy love was all you would experience even if you felt otherwise. She didn't know how true it was and couldn't help but wonder if he had had his heart broken long ago and was doing his best to guard hers instead. Yet this was the real thing, she knew. It had to be.

Rose had crushes before. She knew what it was like to get her stomach all up in a knot over a guy. She knew the thrill of talking to them, holding hands, kissing. But with Zach, all the stuff that had gone on before didn't compare. It was like comparing dreams to reality, and with Zach, it was *real*. It was like her heart had been closed her whole life, its only ability to merely *care* for her friends and family, even guys she gushed about in the past. Zach, though, seemed to crack her heart open and get inside it in a way no one else had. With Zach came visions of the future: dating through college, marriage proposal, a wedding, an unforgettable honeymoon, children.

But there was more to it than that as well. No matter what she said to him, he complimented her every feeling, every statement, even every thought. It was so idyllic—even cliché—that for a while she fought it. Girls dreamed of the fairytale, sure. They all did. But for it to actually come true? To actually find a guy who made her melt every time he was near, whose every word was like heavenly music, whose very look made her want to kiss him—no, this wasn't puppy love.

Puppy love didn't come with heartache, not the kind that made you want to die because the other person wasn't around anymore. Not the kind that turned the person of your dreams into someone of nightmares because they hurt you so bad. Not the kind that became part of every thought, word and deed since they were gone.

The bus pulled up to the stop and Rose got on with the others waiting. It was nearly full, but she managed to find a seat near the back next to a chubby guy in a red golf shirt. He gave her a thoughtful look; she smiled back in kind then looked the other way.

Even when the bus was full she and Zach would find a way to be together, whether it was him standing right next to where she sat or her sitting on his lap despite everyone else's squinty-eyed looks.

The memory made her smile, then made her heart burn with longing.

She wished she could get over it. Wished she could move on enough to not obsess over his vanishing act every two seconds.

Rose blinked away the tears and hugged her backpack tight.

Hopefully the ride home wouldn't take too long.

◆ ◆ ◆

When Rose headed up her driveway, she stopped when she saw Parker sitting on her front steps. He wore a pale blue T-shirt, jeans, his long, rich black hair contrasting against them. She headed up the rest of the driveway and toward the front door.

"Hey," she said.

"Rose," he said with a nod of the head as if tipping an invisible hat. "How goes it?"

"It goes."

"Yeah?" He stood and dusted off the backside of his jeans. "That's cool."

"Didn't see you in school today," she said as she fished out her house key.

"Well, you know me. Late nights and all. I dig the whole sleep thing."

"You're going to sleep your way to being held back a year if you don't get your act together."

"Me? Nah, I'm covered." He came up right behind her. She glanced at him over her shoulder. He took the hint, took a step back and cleared his throat. "Sorry. Listen, there's this thing tonight. A party. Want in?"

"No, thanks."

"What, you're getting all boring on me now?"

"It's not that, it's just—" She stuck the key in the lock, turned it.

"Just what?"

"Just don't feel like going out tonight."

"Oh, come on, man. You've been like a slug in the mud for a few months now. You okay?"

No, I'm not, but thanks for asking. "I'm fine. Just been really bogged down as of late. Schoolwork. You know the drill."

"So says the smartest girl I know."

"Besides, if I did come out, I know you too well and you'll make us stay out late. I'll go to school totally bagged tomorrow, you won't go at all, and I'll have contributed to your—what's the word?—delinquency?"

"Well, fancy pants" —he gave her a wink— "how about I give you a ring later and we'll see how you're doing?"

She shook her head. "You know, I just want to stay in tonight."

"It'll be fun."

She smiled. "I'm sure it will be. Besides, where's it at?"

"Park down the road."

"McIvor?"

"Yeah."

"You know they got guys who walk that place at night, looking for guys like you causing trouble."

"Yeah, and one of 'em Tucker's brother and, actually—" He cupped his hand around his mouth and came in close. With a fake scream hidden in a whisper, he said, "He's coming to the party."

"You're bad."

"You're hot."

She shot him a look.

"Sorry."

"No, I'm sorry." Him giving her compliments was nothing new. If anything, their playful and sometimes flirtatious banter made their friendship lively and fun. She just wasn't in the mood for it today. Besides—and especially now—goofing off with Parker would betray Zach. Zach had been cool with Parker, but never liked how evident Parker swooned over her. She always assured him everything was fine and he had nothing to worry about.

"No worries. So, call later?"

"Not tonight."

"So, call later?"

"I said not tonight."

He backed down the steps and shoved his hands in his pockets. "Right, so I'll call you later."

"I'm not answering," she sang as she started into the house.

"Talk to you later, Rose."

"Bye."

Parker headed down the driveway.

Rose got into the house and closed the door behind her. *He won't let me hear the end of it. He'll call and call and call and call* . . . "Guess I'm going out tonight." *So don't want to.*

5

Marcus Jordan pulled his black SUV up to his house on Valor Road. And even though it technically wasn't just *his* house, but belonged to both him and his wife, Shelly, he still thought of it as such because it was *him* who introduced Shelly to it not long after they were married.

It was *their* home, one separate from the one they shared with their daughter Rose. Years as a bachelor with little living expenses and working as a rookie real estate agent afforded him this place in addition to the one he had on the other side of the city, the house that Rose grew up in. His daughter didn't know about this place, and had no reason to guess of its existence. It was all a matter of schedule and getting his story straight, and with years of practice, him and Shelly had their speeches and routines down cold: work 9-2:30 or 3 P.M. selling houses; 3:30 until 5 or 6 at the second house; then "home" after that, only to return to this place most nights well after Rose had gone to bed. Before Rose was old enough to stay home alone, he and Shelly would alternate nights so one of them was home with her in case they were needed.

Marcus stepped out of the vehicle, went up to the front door, grabbed the junk mail from the box, then entered the six-digit security code on the keypad above the door handle. He went in, dumped the mail on the lacquered oak bench by the door, then proceeded to the kitchen for a cup of coffee. Shelly should be along shortly and they'd have the "Minutes," as he liked to call them, when one would update the other on the previous night's take.

Once the coffee brewed and a cup was poured, Marcus leaned against the countertop and mentally separated himself from his day as a real estate agent to the man he truly was underneath: a vampire slayer.

The cut on his jaw still stung when he opened his mouth wide enough. That rotten punk from last night had gotten a clean shot in with those sharp nails of his before a stake was driven through the young man's heart.

He took another sip, then glanced toward the front door when he heard it open.

His wife clapped twice upon entering, a signal that it was indeed her and not someone who had found out about their secret home.

She entered the kitchen, gave him a kiss on the cheek. She accidentally kissed his cut and he pulled back with a wince.

"Rough night?" she asked, taking his coffee from his hand. He almost didn't notice as he was too lost in her rich brown eyes to pay attention to much else. Even after all these years of being together, Shelly was still his princess and had him wrapped around her little finger. She knew it, too, and sometimes used that soft pouty face she made to get what she wanted.

"Hm?" he said.

She took a sip of his coffee and brushed her auburn hair away from her eyes. "I said, rough night?"

He touched the cut on his face. "Oh this. Yeah, I suppose. Little bloodsucker was quick, quicker than usual. Probably because he was younger when he turned."

"And is he—"

"Yes, done. There were also three others. Two had been together, wandering the Forks, searching for late-night strollers. The third was in the Exchange, probably preying on the homeless."

"Cop out."

"Maybe, but I was only able to take him down. Don't know if he infected anybody or killed them altogether. He had fresh blood around his mouth and the front of his shirt was soaked, so I suspect he had bitten at least one person. Maybe more."

"Seems each one we take down only brings forth others."

He took his coffee back, raised the mug high as if in a toast. "Ah, but if we didn't catch them, they'd be everywhere by now. The city would have been overrun a long time ago." He brought the mug to his lips and took a long, hot sip. The cup was now empty. "Care for more?"

"I'll get my own," she said with a smile, then went to the cupboard and got her own mug. As she prepped her cup, she said, "I'll take tonight. Alone."

"I thought we'd be going together?"

"That was the plan, but I'm worried about Rose. She's taking Zach's disappearance really hard."

"Ah, she'll get over it." He got to work making another cup of coffee for himself.

"Maybe one day, but right now he's all she thinks about."

"Puppy love. She'll be fine." He added a shot of sugar to his coffee. "Besides, how do you know he's all she thinks about? Has she said anything?"

Shelly shook her head. "No, but she doesn't need to. I can see it in her eyes. Half the time she's a million miles away."

"Hm," he said, and tapped the edge of his spoon on the mug's rim. "Want me to talk to her?"

"Maybe, but right now I think it'd be best to just give

her some room and let her do whatever she wants to make herself happy. Safety in consideration, of course."

"Of course."

"It also means we should wait on telling her."

"About us?"

She nodded and brought her mug to her lips.

"Agreed." It had seemed Rose was at the perfect age to be told about her special heritage, was old enough to handle the truth.

The vampire community also seemed to have a code about age. They seemed to slaughter children and drain them of so much blood that turning wasn't possible. Those about thirteen or fourteen and up seemed to be the ones they didn't drain completely. Part of it, Marcus suspected, was teenagers were old enough to make sense of the power they'd inherit and, with guidance, be able to control it much more quickly. Kids and their impulses . . . how many would long for their families and make a spectacle of themselves, flying about the city, climbing up walls, moving at superspeed—it was too much of a risk for the vampires. Right now, their survival depended on their secrecy and operating in the shadows.

In a way, sadly, the slayers were part of the problem despite so desperately trying to be the solution. With the frequency of vampire feedings or turnings, many people went missing as a result. Fortunately, the slayers had people in the hospitals, morgues, government, media, and emergency services. With the right cover story or direct handling of the body, much of what went on never reached the public ear.

Likewise, the undead had certain people in their employ to help provide blood for them, recently deceased corpses, and those with the ability to fudge the details of certain "discrepancies" when it came to the dead.

If it was needed, relatives of the deceased were bought off for their silence. However, the undead, like the slayers, had to be careful with who they dealt with.

If the vampires knew one thing all too well, it was that almost anyone could be a slayer. Not that slayers were common, but having been the protectors of the city since its inception, the slayers were able to have at least one of their team in every major industry, never mind freelancers on the side. Everyone from a mom in the playground all the way to a police officer could be deadly.

Marcus set his mug down. "Time to check inventory."

Shelly nodded, finished her coffee, and the two headed down the stairs, past the family room and to the basement door. Shelly pulled a key from the coiled band around her wrist and stuck it in the lock of the knob. Once open, they went down the flight of stairs and hit the power switch at the bottom. The room lit up, revealing an arsenal of weaponry for their occupation.

Crossbows lined the wall across from them, and below those was a long rack loaded with silver stakes. Silver-bladed swords and machetes lined the wall adjacent, and beneath those, a bin of garlic-laced steam grenades.

There was a door against another wall, locked and chained. If anything, it was their trophy room, a place to store any vampires that didn't disintegrate upon receiving a stake to the heart.

That was the problem with turning: it could be unpredictable and not everyone transformed the same.

In the middle of the room were bullet- and slash-proof his-and-her body armor, worker jumpsuits both light and dark, as well as a rack with hanging utility belts.

Good thing we invested wisely, Marcus thought. Most of the stuff in the room was reasonably affordable. It was all the silver they had to buy that kept the cost up. Usually either him or Shelly would make trips to goldsmiths and jewelry stores and buy the purest silver items they could find. They'd take them back to the secret house and, at the tool station further back in the basement, use their own homemade smelting operation to create the weapons as required. Most of the stuff was reusable, as when a vampire disintegrated on impact, the silver stake would remain behind. However, there were the occasional run-ins that forced them to leave their weapons behind, or if a vampire was stabbed in the leg or arm, the creature would sometimes take off with the weapon. The kicker was, though ordinary wooden stakes would do, the vampire still had a chance to heal if the stake was removed quickly enough. A silver one, however, would poison the bloodstream and the bloodsucker would die regardless, whether right away or a couple hours later.

Shelly was already busy taking her pick of a sword and knife off the wall, while Marcus got her armor ready and began loading the pouches on the utility belt with garlic steam grenades, small knives, cell phone—just for their secret operations—and a few other things.

Though he knew Shelly could handle herself and had demonstrated such many times in the past, he still didn't like the idea of her going out alone.

He prayed nothing would happen to her. Not tonight, not ever.

6

ZACH, TWILIGHT IS upon us," his mother said. She shook him gently on the shoulder.

Zach opened his eyes. He lay in his coffin, its plush lining a cradle to his body. Its heavy stone lid was no longer on top of it, and the wooden ones were open.

"Are you rested?" she asked.

He merely nodded, then sat up. His mother stood upon the stone lid, which was on the floor.

His mother.

Though it was embarrassing to admit, she was beautiful, with perfect pale skin, bright red lips and silky-smooth black hair. Her black dress didn't have a wrinkle on it. Oddly, too, referring to her as his mother seemed natural.

After meeting her this morning, she urged him to get some rest and saw to it he was comfortable in his coffin before mysteriously—and telekinetically—lifting its heavy lid, closing the wooden ones, the stone one sliding into place on top of the stone box. He had asked her why even put the lids on if it was just them inside the tomb.

"For our protection," she had said, "in case a stranger came along during the day. Not only would the daylight streaming in harm us, but in our weakened and exposed state, we might not be able to defend ourselves against them."

Before she had closed the lid, however, she leaned in and gently kissed his mouth. At first, all he wanted to do was scream and get this woman off him, but just as quickly as the impulse came, so did it vanish and the brief peck she gave him was a welcome one. The love, adoration and care that oozed from her kiss was enough to let Zach know in his heart of hearts that everything was going to be okay. She closed the lid and he dreamed.

It began as a nightmare, one where this same woman, who moments ago carefully tucked him in, was tightly gripping his body, her face shoved deep into the crook of his neck. He could barely see what was going on with all her black hair in his eyes. It was all feeling: the entrapment, the strong sense of helplessness, the pain. He remembered two sharp prongs digging deep into his neck, then a moment later the gush of warm blood that leaked out along his shoulder and down his back. The sound of gulping—*her* gulping. The fiery pain in his neck built and built until green stars and black inky whirlpools filled his vision. His body went numb, every muscle locking, the spasms rich and agonizing. He wanted to scream, but he could scarcely open his lips without receiving a mouthful of hair.

The pain took him, spreading from his neck all through his back and shoulders and finally throughout his entire body. He shook, jerked and twisted. Then, finally, release. The pain stopped instantaneously and a rush of darkness swooped into his sight and enveloped him completely.

Moments later, he was back in the coffin, his mother shaking his shoulder.

"I had . . ." he started.

"You remembered," she said.

"It was real?"

"It's always real. Your first dream as one of us. Though you slumbered in your bed, you finished being reborn into our world. The first step is always the dream, the recollection of your change."

He replayed the dream over in his mind's eye, wincing. "I don't remember, um, changing."

"The darkness," she said. "That was when it happened. Though it seemed to you to last only an instant, in fact you were lying among us for several months."

"Several months!" Zach bolted out of the coffin and ran to the center of the crypt.

"Calm down, my son."

"Stop calling me that!"

"But I am your mother." Her voice was innocent, as if she truly believed it.

I believe it, too, he thought. More so, he *knew* it. Yet this lady in front of him was not the woman he identified as "mother." That person was someone else. He just couldn't remember a face or a name.

"What's with all the shouting?" came a gruff voice behind Zach.

He turned around to see a man sitting up in another coffin. The man appeared in his thirties, with black hair and brown eyes like the woman's. He wore a fine suit, but one Zach instinctively knew was out of date, probably by a couple of decades.

"Your son has awoke, my dear," the woman said to the man.

"Ha!" The man jumped out of the coffin, seemed to vanish into thin air for a moment, before reappearing right in front of Zach. "So it is you, my boy. When your mother said she was going to bring you to us, I told her that you might be difficult to find. I guess not. After all, you look just like her."

"What?" Zach said.

"He suffers memory loss, dear, just like Wil had."

The man furrowed his brow. "Oh, I see. Well, no

matter" —he slapped a hand on Zach's shoulder— "you'll come around soon enough."

Zach knew he should run and get away from these people as fast as he could, but his legs seemed locked and his feet glued to the floor.

"Also seems your mother's keeping you here, huh."

"I'm just doing what's best. He can't go running. He's already been out of the tomb," she said.

"Is that so?"

"But he came back, as if he knew this was where he belonged. If he leaves, it will have to be with one of us, or with Wil, maybe Cassie."

"Who's coming with me where?" came another voice.

Zach turned to see the remaining closed coffins in the room were now open. One had a girl, the other a young man. Both seemed to be in their early twenties.

"Wil, Cassandra, I'd like you to meet your brother Zach," his mother said.

The girl was beside him in an instant and wrapped her arms around him. "Finally, finally, we're together. Mom said you were the last to join us. Oh, I have so much to tell you."

"Hush up, Sis," the young man said as he simply strolled over from his own coffin. "The guy just got here and, judging by the look on his face, doesn't have a clue as to what's going on."

"Memory loss," Zach's mother sang softly then looked away.

"Oh, just like me," Wil said. "Cool. I remember what that was like. Scary, weird, yet seeming almost natural. Being here, I mean. That's why you haven't run yet, am I right?"

Looking at Wil was like looking in a mirror. Zach was merely just a younger version with smoother features.

Run? "I can't run."

"No, Mommy dearest is keeping your feet stuck to the ground." Wil leaned in close and whispered, "Don't worry, she did the same thing to me. Cassie, on the other hand, well, she woke up 'intact,' so to speak, and had a complete meltdown until Mom explained everything."

"Yeah, well, no one's perfect," Cassie said, pulling her black hair back in a ponytail and binding it with an elastic band.

Zach thought the plaid-skirted schoolgirl outfit she wore fit beautifully and complimented her in all the right places.

"Dude, she's your sister," Wil said.

"Huh?" Zach said.

Wil tapped his temple with his forefinger. "I can read your thoughts."

"What?"

"Okay, kids, that's enough," the man said. "Look, Zach, I know all this is hard for you to take in. I understand, I really do. Tell you what: this thing goes both ways. We're here for you and will do our best to let you get used to things. But we also need you to listen to what we say and believe what we tell you."

"I don't know what to say."

"You don't have to say anything," the man said, love in his eyes.

"No, that's not what I meant. I don't know *what* to say. I'm standing here without a clue as to what's going on other than I got people standing around me telling me they're my family. I got some woman who can apparently give me weird dreams and keep my feet stuck to the ground. I'm in a tomb, it stinks in here and I'm really, really thirsty." That last statement wasn't meant to come out.

"Has he fed?" the man asked his mother.

"Not yet. Tonight he will. He'll have to as he was entombed for so long."

"Good, I'm hungry," Zach said.

"Wait and see what's on the menu," Cassie said.

The man stuck out his hand. "I'm Rain, your father."

Zach didn't want to take the man's hand, but what felt like an invisible one grabbed him by the wrist and raised his forearm and hand to meet the man's anyway. Rain took his hand and shook it.

Rain said, "And that's Mira, your mother." He finally let go of Zach's hand; Zach snapped it back to his side immediately.

"Did Mother tell you what happened to you?" Wil asked.

"No. Not really. Only that I was in a coffin and something about a 'change' and . . . I can't remember the rest."

Mira came up beside him and put her mouth to his ear. "What once was human is now no more." She leaned in even closer. "Zach, my son, you are a vampire."

7

It was near seven o'clock, and Rose's parents were still not home yet.

Probably another late-night client, she thought.

She sat on her bed cross-legged, a pink shoebox in front of her. She ran the fingertips of one hand along its top, tracing the outline of the red sparkling heart on the lid. Each side also held a heart, a red one made of felt. This was Zach's box, the one he made for her when they exchanged their feelings for one another. She had made a similar one for him. Purple, with a blue felt heart glued to its lid. She had decorated the sides of the box she gave him with tiny silver hearts and diamond stickers, writing "I love you" in different colored markers in and around them. It was in these boxes they decided to keep anything precious they gave to each other.

Heart aching, Rose opened the lid and went through its contents: notes, movie tickets, the bill from their first dinner together, a handmade bracelet, Zach's picture, a stick-figure drawing of them he doodled during chem. class. It was the letter on the bottom she wanted. It was two pages of regular lined loose-leaf, folded in thirds.

She pulled it out, unfolded it, and let her eyes wander the words without really reading it. Right now, she just wanted to see his handwriting, know he once touched the pages.

She set the papers down. "You have to stop doing this to yourself." *He's missing. He didn't leave you. He just . . . vanished.* "What if something happened to him? What if he's . . ." She couldn't say it. To do so would give in to what she feared the most.

Tears welled up at the bottom of her eyes. When she blinked, they ran down her cheeks. "I just really miss you," she whispered.

Rose looked at the first page again, Zach's printing bringing him to life as if he was with her now. Out of all the things in the Heart Box, it was this letter that was the most precious. It was in this letter where he poured his heart out to her.

It read:

Dearest Rose,

What can I say to a girl like you? I've been sitting here thinking how to even start a letter like this. Even just thinking why I'd put all this stuff in a letter to begin with. The truth is, I don't think I could ever say these things to you. Not that I wouldn't want to, but because I know that if I started, I'd probably break down crying like a kid. You know me: I love the mushy stuff, but am just not good at saying it. At least, not in the way I want to right now. Besides, if I write it down, then you'll have something to read later if you want to hear it again.

So, yeah, how to start? What can I say that doesn't come off cheesy, or even stupid?

I'll just be honest, and who cares what comes out. Just gonna roll with my heart on this one. I hope you're okay with that.

I love you, Rose. I really, really love you. I mean, when we first started dating, I thought I loved you. I was excited all the time, each thought of you making me smile. Couldn't wait to see you in between classes and after school. But somewhere along the way, all that stuff faded and a new world opened up to me. You became more real, more authentic, more intimate to me.

I go crazy when you're not around, so much so that I get scared.

Especially at night when I'm alone in my bed. When I lie there thinking of you, I can't sleep my heart aches so much. I sometimes imagine my pillow is you and I take it in my arms and hug it tight (even kiss it sometimes, as goofy as that sounds).

When I see you in the morning a sudden rush of relief washes over me and I know I have the strength to face one more day.

I'm excited, sure, but now the excitement is over where we can go with our relationship. Like I said, I get scared because I've fallen utterly and completely in love with you. You're such a part of me now that the very thought of us not being together—for whatever reason—makes me feel like I've lost a part of myself. The incompleteness is so overwhelming that I think I'm having a heart attack. Then I remember you and that we're together. Then I'm okay.

Everything is okay.

The touch of your skin, the way your hand fits perfectly into mine—the way you give it the occasional squeeze when we're walking . . . it sends electricity through me. All I want is to just pick you up, hold you and kiss you and tell you that I love you.

Those three little words—those three life-changing words—are all I want to say. Even when I'm alone I think of you and out loud I keep saying I love you. I just need to tell you, you know? Need to get it off my chest and fill your ears with those special words because no matter what happens or where life takes us, I deeply want you to know that I love you and that I always will. That you can always count on me. I won't be perfect. No one can be. But I'll be the best guy in your life, if you keep me around. I'll try my hardest for that, and if I mess up, if I somehow let you down, please know that even now I'm heartbreakingly sorry and will try my best to never screw up again.

When I kiss you, Rose, your lips are delicious. Not just physically, but emotionally, too, because through our kisses I can feel everything you feel about me. There's fire between us. Red, hot scorching fire that blows me away every time I think about what you and I have.

I could drink of your lips forever. I really could because if I did, then that's like me telling you a zillion times over that I love you and that you mean the world to me.

I'd do anything for you, Rose. Anything. There's nothing I wouldn't do.

I'd die for you. Even a thousand times if it came to it. Any amount of pain or torment, if it somehow was tied to your happiness, if it could somehow express how I feel about you, yes, absolutely, I'd do it for you.

And I want to thank you for—and here's where it might get weird—you and I abstaining from, well, you know. We've both said that at times it's been hard, but I also think that, at least right now, it's a good call. I've been thinking about it and what I think is happening is because we don't do that stuff, we grow closer together despite others maybe arguing that you-know-what is the be-all and end-all of intimacy. Sure, I agree with that, in a way, but I also know that because that's not what we do, we then have to express ourselves to each other in other ways. All those looks you give me, the hugs, handholding, notes, kisses, late night phone calls, morning phone calls, surprise letters in my mailbox, in my binder—it really deepens things.

I've never known anything like this before and my hope and prayer is that I never will again, meaning that what I have with you is all I want. You're all I want. You're all I need.

You're the greatest, Rose. You've changed my life and given me a reason for living.

I just love you so, so, so much that I want to tell you again and again.

I love you!

I love you!

I love you!

Rose, my dearest Rose, I love you.

Yours forever and always,

Zach

Ps. I love you! (Sorry, had to say it again.)

Rose set the pages down and let the tears fall. "I love you, too, Zach, forever and always."

"**Y**OU DIDN'T CALL her, did you?" Marcus said as he went to drop Shelly off downtown. His wife wore a long overcoat, concealing her armor and weapons.

"I thought you did?"

"No, I thought you did." *So much for being an expert at secrecy.*

"Great. Now she's probably wondering what's going on."

"Probably just assuming we have a late-night showing or something. Wouldn't be the first time."

"I hate all this hiding!"

"I know. Me, too, but right now it has to be done. You've said as much before yourself."

She glanced over at him. "Like the saying goes: 'Easier said than done.'"

"No kidding." He drove Shelly up to the far side of the Exchange District, where it ran along the river. Aside from the light from the condos lining the street across the way, the river side was dark, the trees dividing the road from the river even darker. It was a perfect place to begin their hunt. "Use the cell phone if you need anything."

"Likewise you."

"You ready?"

"Always am. Besides, seems around here is a favorite spot for the bloodsuckers."

She was right. The trees lining the river were thick and dark enough that they made a perfect place for someone without a home to spend the night. It was safe there, away from the sidewalks and streets, and if you built your shelter on the river side, it was too dangerous for anyone to come calling.

Unless that person had nothing to fear. Unless they were a vampire.

He pulled the vehicle up to the curb. Shelly leaned in and gave him a kiss. "Love you."

"Love you, too."

She exited the vehicle and, as was their rule, didn't look back as he pulled away, one small thing they did to change modes and get to work.

Marcus hoped she would be safe tonight.

♦ ♦ ♦

The phone rang and Rose answered, wiping away the tears.

"Hey, it's Parker. Told you I'd call."

"As if you wouldn't," she said, replacing the lid on the Heart Box.

"You coming out tonight?"

She really didn't feel like it. Not that she was tired or anything, but even the simple act of going out with friends had lost its luster recently. She looked at the box and could envision Zach's letter lying within. Reading it soothed her aching heart, but once she was done, the sharp pain inside her chest ignited anew.

"I'm not sure," she said. "Was thinking of staying in."

"I know. You told me as much earlier. But I really think it'd do you some good."

Do me some— "Really?"

"What, you don't think I know you're down in the dumps? Zach was a cool guy and I'm just as concerned as you are as to what happened to him."

As if he could be. Parker had no idea. "Yeah, well, it just hasn't been easy with him being gone and all."

"I know. I'm not trying to make you forget about him or anything." His voice went soft, gentle. "Just want to see you smile again. Sometimes you just need to get out of the house, you know? Sitting there moping might seem like a good idea, but coming out, getting some air and just talking crap with folks—even just with me—might be what the doctor ordered."

"Okay, doc," she said, a little bit of snark to her tone.

"Come on, it'll be fun."

She thought about it for a moment: it was either sit alone in the house until whenever her folks got home, or take a chance and maybe mute the pain for a few hours. "Tell you what . . . I'll come out, but if at any time I want to go, you'll stand by me on that, okay?"

"I'll stick by you no matter what." And he meant it. His tone said it all. If Parker was anything, he was loyal.

"Okay."

"I'll come get you in twenty minutes or so."

"You got your license back?"

"Yeah. The old man saw fit to give me another chance."

"Did he fix the car?"

"Not yet, but he's still letting me drive it."

She knew how pissed his dad had been when Parker came home with a busted taillight. "As long as you don't smash it up with me in it, I'll even let you open the door for me."

"Deal. See you in a bit."

"Later."

"Ta ta," he sang.

Smiling, she hung up the phone. She headed to her closet. She needed something to wear. Preferably black to signify her somber mood.

♦ ♦ ♦

Marcus got home a little after nine. After dropping Shelly off, he had to swing by the post office, get some gas and a jug of milk from the store. He took his shoes off, went to the kitchen and flicked the light on. There was a note on the kitchen table.

Out with Parker and some friends. Won't be out late. Just needed some air.

Rose

"Better not be late," he said. "Tonight's a school night."

No sooner than he put the jug of milk in the fridge did his cell phone ring.

"Hello?" he said.

"It's me," Shelly said, panting. "The river's a hotspot. Already dispatched two bloodsuckers, but I have another two on my tail. Who knows how many more are afoot. Need you out here now."

"On my way." He darted out of the kitchen, put his shoes on, then doubled back. He scribbled a note under Rose's telling her he had to check something at the office. "She's going to hate me for this." He dropped the pen, ran to the door, locked up, then jumped in the SUV.

As he tore off down the street to meet his wife, he ran mental inventory on the hidden arsenal in a compartment in the trunk. It held a collapsible stab-proof vest, two silver, foot-long blades, three spikes and one garlic steam grenade. It was meant for emergencies only, and judging by the urgency in his wife's voice, this sure sounded like one.

9

Zᴀᴄʜ ꜱᴀᴛ ɪɴ the corner of the crypt alone, while the others sat on his mother's coffin in the middle of the room, talking quietly amongst themselves. He had thought about running, but instead chose to stay put here in the crypt. As unsettling as all this was, something deep within kept him here and it wasn't anything his mother forced upon him. The more time passed, the more the air of familiarity about these people grew. He *had* known them before, but, he felt, it had been a long time ago. Years, even. From where or when he knew them, he didn't know, and something else inside said he had known *others* between when he first knew this strange family until he met them now.

She had called me a vampire, he thought. He had checked for fangs already, but there were none. He also noticed the others didn't have them either. Rain had told him the fangs were for feeding only and ran more on instinct than anything else.

Vampire. Though he'd already mulled the word over a million times, it still seemed unbelievable, but at the same time, wholly possible, even plausible.

The way he felt, the energy swelling within, the paleness of his skin, this strange thirst which he was told would not be quenched by water—it made sense. Not to mention the spontaneous combustion in direct sunlight. In his head, he had already accepted the truth, but in his heart, the place where real decisions and beliefs were made, it still refused to side with this bizarre family.

"I know you're doubting," Mira said, suddenly sitting next to him.

Zach knew he should have been startled, but he wasn't.

"I can make you believe, but you need to trust me," she said.

"How?"

"Ooh, can I take him?" Cassie said, suddenly at his side as well. "You took Wil, Mom. Let me take Zach."

"Take me where?"

Mira simply smiled. "Up."

Cassie pulled Zach to his feet by the hands. Her strength was incredible. With a huge grin she said, "You're going to love this."

She led him by the hand and the two made their way up the crypt's stone steps to the door leading to the mausoleum proper. Once through, Zach glanced at the stacked coffins and wondered if these folks were vampires, too. Once out in the graveyard, he was surprised at how clearly he saw in the dark. Each tombstone was bright gray, the shadows stretching out across the grass as black as pitch. The bark of the trees dotting the rows of the dead was as crisp and clear as if he was looking at them in broad daylight.

"Ready?" Cassie said, obviously eager for something.

He furrowed his brow. "Ready for what?"

She giggled.

Suddenly, Wil burst through the mausoleum's door, his face beaming as well. "I don't want to miss this."

Soon Mira and Rain were standing outside the door with him. "Neither do we," Rain said. "A vampire's first flight is a special occasion."

First flight? Zach thought.

"Yes, first flight," Cassie said. She gave him a wink.

"We can read minds, too, remember?"

Zach looked to Wil. Wil said, "It's true. You will, too. Took me awhile but it eventually came." After a pause. "Kind of annoying in crowded places, though. Still learning how to turn it off and on."

Zach bit his lip, half-expecting to bite through the flesh, but then remembered that right now there were no fangs in his mouth.

"Don't listen to him," Cassie said. "You ready?"

"I don't even know what to say right now," Zach said.

"Just say yes."

"Okay, um, yes?"

"Now click your heels and say, 'There's no place like the sky. There's no place like the sky.'"

"What?"

"Cassie!" Mira's voice was like ice. To Zach, "Pay her no mind, my son. She's just excited."

"I see."

Cassie took his hand in hers. "Sorry. It's really not that hard. You just need to understand that you *can* do this. That's the key. You. Can. Do. This. Now, close your eyes."

He did. "Now what?"

No answer.

"Cassie?" Zach opened his eyes. He was in the sky, the earth below hidden by clouds beneath his feet.

Screaming, he flailed his arms, toppled backward in the air and began to fall. Wind rushed by him. Everything went gray-white as he fell through the clouds, then suddenly he watched as those same clouds grew further and further away as he tumbled toward the earth.

"Close your eyes," a female voice shouted from next to him. Cassie floated over him, somehow keeping herself in the air just above him even as he fell. "You need to relax."

Zach could only scream.

"Zach! Do you want to die?"

His eyes went wide.

"Shut 'em!"

He squeezed his eyes shut, expecting at any moment for the sudden impact of hitting the ground.

The wind stopped whistling by his ears. The ground never came.

"Open your eyes," Cassie said.

He did. He was on his back, hovering some fifty feet or so above the earth, the cemetery tombstones like gray pebbles below him. "How?"

"It's instinct . . . but you need to relax. Closing your eyes helps. Fools your brain into removing yourself from what's really going on by removing sight. You still know you're falling, but with that momentary calmness in the mind, it allows your survival instinct to take over and stop your descent."

He absorbed the moment. Hovering there, it was like floating in water. There was substance beneath him, but nothing nearly as solid as the ground. It was a cushion of air. It was freedom.

"How—" He started and leaned forward. His body did ninety degrees and he went upright. "How did I get so high so fast?"

Cassie floated close beside him. The two hung there in the air like ornaments on a tree. "Mom telekinetically gave you a boost a few feet up. Your body recognized what was going on and so your own flight ability kicked in. How you got up here so fast? Speed. Pure speed— which is pretty awesome, I might add. One of my favorite parts since rebirth."

"Speed? Like superfast motion?"

"Kind of. More like a combination of actual speed and teleportation. From what I've seen from the others and from what I can do myself, you basically start at one point, superspeed to a point a few feet from where you started, then suddenly teleport to where you want to be. Then, when you appear there, you superspeed a few more feet before stopping. It's really quite a thrill and I can't wait until you try it for yourself."

"My heart should be racing," he said. As cool as floating here above the cemetery was, the expected exhilaration he wanted to feel wasn't there. He put a hand to his chest. "No heartbeat."

"Why would there be?" Cassie said. "You're dead . . . well . . . undead."

10

MARCUS SPED TO the spot along the river where he dropped his wife off a couple hours before. He turned the vehicle off, got out, ran around to the back and threw open the trunk. He unlocked the secret compartment beneath the trunk floor and immediately armed himself in the stab-proof vest, slid silver-plated swords into the sheaths, strapped a knife and the stakes to his leg, and put the garlic steam grenade in his pocket. After slamming the trunk down, he ran into the woods, pulling his cell phone out. He speed-dialed Shelly.

"Pick up, pick up, pick up," he said.

She did. "You here?"

"Where are you?"

"Same side of the river you dropped me off, heading north." A growl came over the line somewhere in the distance. "Keep your ears open. These guys are good."

"Roger. I'm coming, sweetie. Stay alive."

Marcus picked up his speed and headed into the thick of the trees, weaving around tree trunks, hopping over bushes, ducking low behind others; he thought he heard something.

The wind rustled the leaves, and he thought he picked up movement up ahead. He stopped and quickly scanned the darkness. The sound ceased, so he kept his ears open and waited a moment. When he heard nothing else, he continued on his path through the trees. Something hard caught his foot and he went tumbling face first to the ground. Immediately upon impact, he rolled over and got to his feet.

Someone stood before him: short-cropped brown hair, pale skin, black-lined eyes. The young man wore a tight black T-shirt and black jeans. The man's long fingernails confirmed what he was.

"I ask you, mate," the young man said, his voice smooth, British. "Why do you hunt in the night?"

Don't answer. Don't give him an inch. It's just a distraction, Marcus thought. It was a common tool among vampires. The one in front of him was speaking while most likely others lurked somewhere in the shadows around him. Marcus wasn't worried about holding his own. He had a black belt in Aikido, was a second degree in Ninjitsu, and years of fighting with swords and knives trained him to be a formidable foe with weaponry.

"I see," the young man said. "You're here for the female. She's dead!"

Liar. Marcus withdrew both swords and held them aloft in each hand.

The young man wiggled his fingers. "Ooohh, scary." He took a step closer. "So, which number are you? Forty-seven? Thirty-nine? One hundred and eighteen? Doesn't matter. Your kind are no match for us."

Marcus was Slayer Twenty-one. Shelly was Thirty-two. It was how those higher in the Order kept track of who was on the field and who had died in service. If a slayer's life was claimed, their number was crossed out, never to be replaced. The only time the numbers reset themselves was when a new generation of slayers replaced the old. Thousands came before him throughout the centuries.

"I don't have time for this," Marcus said and advanced toward the young man.

Immediately, the man's fists shot out in front of him

and his feet left the ground. He flew straight at Marcus. The moment the man moved, Marcus stepped to the side and brought his sword down as the man flew past. The young man's body dropped to the ground, his head rolling along the forest floor a few feet away. A quick plunge of the sword to the young vampire's heart and the undead creature was finished.

Three more vampires appeared in a semi-circle around him, materializing from the shadows. They were all female, blonde, and beautiful. Each wore a different colored long coat: cherry red, royal blue and snow white.

They hissed and raised their razor-sharp fingernails, ready to maul him like a pack of wild tigers. Quickly, their gorgeous faces went stark white, their features distorting as bone and muscle relocated themselves beneath their skin. The women's brows protruded from their faces as their eyes sunk into their sockets. Their open mouths grew long and their teeth grew as well, giving birth to sharp fangs. Low, guttural growls escaped their lips.

"Come and get it," Marcus said, then realized how corny that sounded.

The girls darted toward him, displacing their bodies from the physical then quickly appearing next to him. The girl in red reached for his neck. In a blur of silver, he removed her arm, turned, and slammed the second blade home into her stomach. With a quick yank upward, he cleaved her in two, straight up her torso, through her neck and head. Marcus withdrew the sword and stuck it deep into the left half of the woman's body, ensuring the heart had been penetrated. He knew he hit his mark when the torso halves erupted into a spray of flesh before disintegrating in the air as fine ash on the wind.

The lady in blue and the one in white were on him immediately. One pulled his legs out from under him and he hit the ground on his back. The other kicked him in the head then knelt down beside him, mouth wide, ready to feed. The girl in blue crawled up his body from by his legs like a mutated spider. He stuck the sword in her forehead, jerked the blade, and threw her to the side. The woman flailed on the ground as she tried to withdraw the blade from her skull. The one in white moved in to bite his neck. Marcus shot his fist into her face, careful to hit her between the eyes and not in the mouth lest he risk getting infected. With the remaining sword, he brought it down in an arc and slammed it home into her neck. Red, coagulated blood gushed out.

He got to his feet. The woman in blue nearly had the blade out. He drove his heel into the butt of the sword and sent the blade into the woman's brain again. She fell on her back; he jumped on her, removing his knife from the sheath on his leg in the process. A quick plunge of the silver metal to the woman's heart and her body disintegrated before him.

Only the lady in white remained. She hissed and growled as she removed the blade from her throat. She came at him, sword held high. His blade met hers in a clash of silver. He kicked her in the gut, sent her stumbling back a few steps, then swiftly closed the distance and drove the sword through her heart. With a shriek, her body exploded like a whirl of snow before disappearing altogether.

Marcus took a deep breath, mentally regrouped, then gathered up his weapons. Shelly was around here somewhere. Though he knew better than to trust a bloodsucker, he just hoped he wasn't too late.

11

"I THOUGHT YOU said we were going out?" Rose asked Parker. The two sat on the sofa of Parker's pal Rick's place.

"I don't know, did I?"

"I think so."

"Why, what's wrong?"

Rick's rec room had eight people in it: five guys, three girls. Rose didn't know any of them except Parker.

"I've never been here before," she said.

"You need a drink," he said and took a swig of beer.

"Don't really feel like one."

"Why not?"

"It's, um . . ." She didn't want to admit she'd never drank before, at least nothing outside the occasional glass of wine her dad sometimes let her have on Thanksgiving or Christmas.

"Oh, come on. You're a booze virgin? I know you're the other kind, but—"

"Parker!"

"Sorry." He looked at his bottle. "Not me talking."

"Yeah, right." She crossed her arms.

Some guy across the room standing next to the pool table shouted at them, "Hey, P., you getting in on this? Mike said he could take me on calls."

"In a minute," Parker said with a raise of his finger.

Rose leaned closer to him. "I just don't know anyone and I didn't really plan on coming out anyway." She hated being a party pooper, but Parker had pulled a fast one on her and wasn't clear about what was going down tonight.

He seemed to consider her words. "Tell you what: let me watch this game then I'll take you home."

"How much have you had to drink?"

"I don't know, three, four?"

"And if you get pulled over?"

He scrunched his face. "I won't get pulled over, you kidding? Cops are stretched thin as it is. No time for routine traffic stops. Besides, they mostly do that on holidays and there ain't one for a while."

She sighed. "Thanks anyway, but I'll head 'er home on my own. Don't want to take a chance."

"Going to call Daddy?"

"Okay, I'm done," she said and stood from the couch. "See ya."

"I'll be here."

From across the room: "Parker! You deaf? Let's go!"

Rose made her way to the stairs, ignoring the looks everyone gave her as she did.

Just want to go home, pour a hot bath, and relax. "Parker's an idiot," she muttered. *Just a couple too many and he sometimes says things he doesn't mean. Can only imagine what comes out of his mouth when he's really hammered.* She put on her shoes and headed out the door.

Going down the driveway, she looked up at the night sky. It was partly cloudy; the sky that was exposed was crystal clear. It reminded her of late night walks with Zach. He was out there somewhere. He was still considered a missing person. His family was in hysterics at first, but now spent every day on edge, wondering if the next phone call would be news about their son. She didn't check in often with them anymore, not that she didn't want to, but even calling there was painful. Dialing that phone number, like she had so many times before to talk to Zach, speaking to his father, the old ideas of one day them being her in-laws—it was too much. She really hoped and prayed they were okay, though. They deserved better than to wonder where their son was, or if he was alive or . . . "Dead," she said without meaning to.

The air was cool, but not uncomfortable. She knew the way home. It would take a good forty minutes to get there. She pulled out her cell phone and dialed home, feeling a bit of a goon for needing Daddy to come to the rescue. The line rang and rang. Eventually, the machine kicked in.

"Great," she said. "Where are you guys?"

She hung up.

Rick lived in the suburbs like she did and, from what she knew, the streets were safe. Very seldom did anything happen.

Just got to stop thinking about Zach. Think about something else, like school tomorrow. "Okay, so not meant that last part." She glanced over her shoulder. "Stupid Parker. Hope he's having a good time."

12

"**I** CAN'T BELIEVE how awesome this is!" Zach said as he and Cassie flew through the air.

"I know. So awesome. Nothing up here but us and, well, sometimes other vamps but, you know, whatever. It's just a chance to relax. Could never do this in the old life."

"Duh." Zach had to admit, he was really enjoying himself. Who wouldn't? Right now, he was thankful he didn't remember anything from his old life. He was even thankful for what he'd become, except: "I'm thirsty, Cassie. Real bad. Mouth is dry. And . . ." How could he explain it? *Just say it even if it sounds stupid. If she's like you, she might understand.* "I feel this kind of dark thing within me. This anger. I have this mental picture of my thirst, and it's black and it carries those feelings with it. I think about something else, and those feelings are gone though I'm still thirsty."

"I know what you mean," she said. She flew over him and came down on his other side. "You haven't fed yet. It's the only downside to being one of us. Well, not really a downside because once you've fed for the first time, you want to be thirsty all the time just so you could do it again."

"What do we eat?"

"*Drink.* Blood. Human blood."

"Blech. No thanks."

"Trust me, it's good stuff. Real good. And it's not even the taste that's good about it, though that's really awesome, too. So yummy." She floated in closer.

"Can I tell you something?"

"About blood?"

She chuckled. "No, about the *feeling*."

"Um, okay."

She gave him a sly grin. "It's like having an orgasm."

He wrinkled his face. "I so don't want to hear this."

"No, you do."

"No, I don't."

He adjusted his flight path so he was further away.

Cassie flew in close to him again. "Just hear me out because it's actually important. Sorta. It *is* like having an orgasm, but full-body, and not even that—though that's super awesome wicked—but it's like that ultra intense kind, the one that hurts but feels amazing at the same time."

"I wouldn't know."

"As if."

"Okay, I do, but not in the way you think."

"As if I don't know what you're talking about. Anyway, it's like the kind where you build up to it, back off, build up to it, back off—and eventually you explode. But imagine that for not just, like, six or seven seconds, but for as long as you feed. Totally euphoric."

"Thanks for the sex class, Sis."

"I'm serious. Besides, you need the blood" —she flew in right up to him again— "if you want to live." Cassie banked to the left and descended into the clouds below. She disappeared from sight.

Zach stopped and hovered in the air. The thirst was getting to him. The darkness was growing. "I'm going to hate this," he said and dove down in Cassie's direction.

When he emerged beneath the clouds, he found Mira waiting for him.

"Where's Cassie?" he asked.

"I sent her away. Your first feed belongs to me."

13

MARCUS RAN THROUGH the woods. "Shelly?" he whispered as loud as he could, doing his best not to attract attention to himself, but if he knew the vampires for what they were, they were probably hunting *him* even now.

Swords drawn, ready to strike down anything that came into his path, he scanned in between the trees and above the bushes for his wife. She had to be here. The patch of trees lining the river would be at an end soon. Unless . . . unless she was the other way.

Can only do one thing at a time, he thought.

He burst through a thicket of bushes and skidded to a halt. A row of a half dozen vampires stood before him, three male, three female, all seeming to have been in their late thirties when they were turned.

The row of the undead eyed him coolly, each gaze like ice, penetrating into his own.

Clear your mind. Don't let them read—

"We know who you are, Marcus, Slayer Twenty-one," the center male said. He wore a snug blue T-shirt, black pants, icy-blond spiked hair, and a studded leather band around his neck.

"Let's cut him open and bleed him dry," the female standing next to the center male said.

"In due time, my dear, but I think he's here looking for his wife."

Shelly . . .

"Yes, 'Shelly,' your darling partner, your soul mate."

Marcus took a step forward, swords at the ready.

The vampire in the center merely held his gaze.

Show her to me, Marcus thought, knowing full well his mind was being read.

"And if I don't?"

"I'll gut you and your friends."

The man with spiked hair glanced side-to-side. "You're outnumbered. Why, even now we could be on you faster than you could move your blade."

"Don't count on it. Now, give me my wife!"

To his comrades, the spiky-haired vampire said, "You heard him. Stand aside."

The six vampires parted down the middle, three to each side, revealing Shelly behind them, gagged, blindfolded and bound to a tree.

They knew one person wouldn't be enough to satisfy them. That's why they lured me here. If I wasn't here, they might eliminate each other in a feeding frenzy.

"No need to explain it to us, Marcus," a pale-skinned woman with pitch black hair said.

"Shelly?" Marcus asked.

She muffled a response.

Marcus sized up his targets, calculating his next move. This wasn't the time for debate as negotiations with vampires rarely yielded any ground. He had to act swiftly, but also had to be ready for them to pounce on him as well.

He needed a distraction. *If you release her, I will look the other way for the next six nights, one for each of you. You will be free to roam as you see fit.* Knowing his mind was being read, his thoughts considered, he lunged forward, throwing his blades out to either side, penetrating the hearts of the nearest two vampires to his left and right. They both shrieked and their bodies exploded in a cloud of fleshy ash that lingered on the air a moment before disappearing altogether.

He hook kicked the next in line on his right, sending the girl back and buying himself a couple precious seconds. Immediately the three remaining undead disappeared from sight and materialized around him, their bodies a scant inch or two from his. He head-butted the spiky-haired man in front of him, back kicked the one he hook kicked to the head because she was already moving toward him, then kicked off the undead man to his side, giving himself some room. The undead man ran at him. Marcus shot out his sword and penetrated the man's chest, killing him instantly. The body disintegrated.

The spiky-haired vampire and a girl with brown hair in ringlets and the one with black hair remained. The brunette hissed at him. He swung out a hook punch. She dodged, grabbed his arm and threw him to the ground with such force the impact put him in a momentary daze. Marcus rolled onto his back just as the girl pounced on him.

"Hold still!" she shrieked.

Shelly muffled somewhere behind the blond, spiky-haired vampire.

Marcus snapped out his fist and punched the girl in the chest. She rocked back a moment and when she rocked forward again, he already had the garlic steam grenade in his hand. Her mouth wide, she went for his neck. He shoved the grenade in her mouth as far as he could and pulled the pin. She shrieked, garlic-scented steam pouring out the sides of her lips as the skin on her head began to sizzle like bacon in a pan. Marcus pushed her off him and came face-to-face with the one with black hair. Immediately, he sent his sword through her heart. She burst into ash. A second later, he was arrested around the throat by the blond vampire. If the undead pressed any harder, his neck would snap, but he knew the vampire would keep him alive to make his blood all the more sweeter. The pressure on his neck so intense, he dropped his swords and grabbed the vampire's wrists so he could wrestle himself free. Hurled into the woods, Marcus broke his fall by twisting to the side and landing on a bush.

He flailed his arms and legs as they tried to find purchase against the thin branches.

The blond-haired vampire roared, his face now distorted into a twisted visage of displaced bone and muscle. Bright white fangs protruded prominently from the devil's mouth. Swords now on the ground behind the blond, Marcus put up his fists. The vampire charged him, disappearing from several feet away and materializing with his arms around Marcus's waist. In an instant, his feet left the ground and the vampire took to the air, flying Marcus between the trees and to the river beyond.

Wind gathering around him, Marcus called for Shelly, then the icy cold of the river struck his back then enveloped him completely.

The cold water shocking his every muscle, Marcus did his utmost to cling to the vampire despite the undead's efforts to let go and retreat to the surface.

In his head, the deathly cold voice of the creature said: *Tonight you pay for the suffering you've inflicted on us all these years.*

Marcus decided not to respond despite all urges to. With his right arm he clung as tightly as he could to the vampire, while with the other reached for the knife strapped to his leg.

The water pressure pressed in upon his ears; a sharp pain grew in his head the further he went down.

Time was running out.

16

"We try and not disturb the humans as much as we can," Mira said as she and Zach flew. "Your father will explain more at the appropriate time, but when it comes to feeding, you cannot do as you please. We have rules, both as a species and as a family. We try to keep our feeding operation as quiet as possible so as to not notify those who would rather see us dead."

"Who's that?" Zach said. He kept his eyes forward, not yet comfortable enough to look around too much while flying. Last time he tried looking at his mother when she spoke, he veered off course and bumped into her.

"They call themselves 'slayers.' We call them a nuisance. They view us as animals that need to be contained. What they fail to realize is that, unlike animals, we operate on even better mental faculties than they do. Our feeding is for our survival. However, like animals, we prey on others to survive. Humans don't stop other animals from feeding upon each other. They only stop humans ending the lives of humans. Likewise for us ending human lives. What you need to know, my son, is that what we do isn't murder no more than a man killing a fatted calf so he can eat is murder. We live off their blood. In return, we do not slaughter all but instead bring them into our fold, as was the case with you, giving them power and immortality. It is a fair exchange, if you want my opinion."

"And there is nothing else we can feed on?"

"Not in terms of survival, no. Yes, we can eat like the humans do. We even enjoy the same food humans do. But to survive, we need their blood. They can produce hemoglobin, we cannot. By ingesting their blood, we absorb what their blood carries and so survive."

Zach wasn't sure drinking blood was such a good idea, but after what Cassie said about how good it felt, he was fine with giving it a try. What guy wouldn't?

"There, below," Mira said and arced her flight downward.

Zach followed her lead and the two landed in a forested area alongside a river.

"It is here we sometimes come for our meal. You see, there are humans without homes who live here. By preying on them and removing any evidence of our involvement, it helps keep our feeding operation quiet. Because those dying are usually without family, even friends, their removal goes more often than not unnoticed and, as a result, slayers aren't notified of their deaths through the various channels they are tuned in to."

"Are you saying slayers are everywhere?"

"No, but they are *aware* regarding most facets of human society."

"Are slayers human?"

"Yes."

"Then why don't you kill them?"

"Because, at present, they outnumber us significantly and have influence in the world of men that we do not. They are also immune to daylight, which we are not."

Like before, when the sun hurt me, he thought.

"Yes. You cannot go out into the sun any more than a rock can swim."

"Why not?"

"No more questions. Your father will fill you in on

more later. You've already learned so much since you've awoken with us." Mira sniffed the air. "Come this way. I smell a human."

Zach followed her through the trees, past bushes, all the while finding it amazing that with each of their footfalls, they scarcely made a sound.

Soon they emerged through another set of trees. Mira said, "Look what's happened." She pointed to the tree in front of them, and despite it being dark, every single detail was clear. A woman was tied to the tree, bound, blindfolded and gagged. She wore a long coat which was partly open, revealing some kind of dark, thick outfit beneath.

Mira approached her, but said to Zach, "Watch where you step." Two silver swords lay on the ground. "Do not touch them." She then added into his mind: *One cut can bring disaster.*

They approached the woman. Her scent—a combination of vanilla perfume and the rich, coppery smell of the blood coursing through her veins—sent the image of Zach's thirst before his eyes, along with the darkness and rage that accompanied it.

The woman moaned something from behind the gag.

"Interesting, very interesting," Mira said, walking her fingers up the woman's face. "You're not going to scream, now, are you, if I remove the gag?"

The woman didn't respond.

"Are you!"

She shook her head.

"Good. If you make a single sound, I will pluck out your tongue and put a hole in your throat. Am I clear?"

It took a moment, but the woman nodded.

Zach envisioned silky red blood gushing from a wound in the woman's neck. He went right up to her, his tongue aching to lick her skin.

"Soon, my son, soon." Mira removed the woman's gag. "It seems something went terribly wrong tonight, didn't it?"

"Yes," the woman flatly said.

"Were you alone?"

"Yes."

"Are you sure?"

"Yes."

Mira looked at Zach and mouthed the words, "She's lying."

How does she kn—

In reply, Mira spoke into his mind: *Do you not hear the blood pumping through her veins? Do you not hear it racing through her body?*

Zach listened. Low, rapid pulses of fluid filled his ears. "I do."

"Let me show you, my son, the punishment for lying."

The woman's body went stiff. "I am ready. Your victory tonight is but a small loss for us. It has been an honor serving in the war against vermin such as you."

"Tsk, tsk," Mira said, "strong words for someone who is about to die. And, yes, tonight you will die. I will not give you the honor of becoming one of us, though, I suppose, that would be a worse fate for you, would it not?"

The woman closed her mouth. Zach saw the muscles in her jaw tighten.

"Come here, my son," Mira said.

He came beside her.

"What you want is this thick artery here," she said, pointing to it on the neck. "Breach that, and you can drink until she is no more." Suddenly, Mira's face distorted; her brow protruded from her skull; her cheekbones rose high on her face, nearly bursting through her skin; her mouth opened wide, revealing inch-long razor sharp teeth. She clamped her mouth around the woman's neck. The woman let out a gasp, then screamed, her cries distorted by the blood bubbling in her throat.

A wave of excitement passed through Zach, the darkness within growing stronger until fire lit up his face as the bones and muscles beneath his skin realigned themselves for the feeding to come.

◆ ◆ ◆

Marcus nearly lost control of the knife when the vampire jerked its body to the side. His eyes were closed. His lungs pounded in need of air. The pain in his head was now in his temples. He envisioned tiny screwdrivers driving into his skull on either side of his eye sockets.

With as hard a thrust as he could muster, he plunged the knife into the vampire's chest. He yanked it out and stabbed it again. He did it a third time and the vampire's flailing ceased.

Got him. Frantically, Marcus headed toward the surface.

◆ ◆ ◆

Zach needed to drink. "Mother, please," he said, catching himself calling her "mother" for the first time since they met.

Mira withdrew from the woman's neck, blood running down her chin. With a hiss, she nodded in the woman's direction.

Instinct took over. It was as if some outside force

guided Zach's mouth to the precise spot on the woman's neck where he needed to be. Maybe his mother was helping. It didn't matter. He had to partake.

He wrapped his mouth around the woman's neck, then bit down, his fangs filling the holes Mira created. His mother's fingers wrapped themselves on either side of his lips and guided them to make a seal around the wound, locking the blood in. The moment the blood hit Zach's tongue, an electrifying pulse shot through him. Bright blue stars danced before his vision as his entire body rode waves of pure pleasure with each gulp of blood. He sucked and swallowed, losing himself in the moment, letting go of the present and falling into eternity. There was no time in this place of feeding. Just utter, body-shaking pleasure. His knees buckled with each wave of euphoria. Mind-blowing surges of joy and pain shot through every muscle in his body. Orgasm after orgasm, his body convulsed as he sucked the blood from the woman's neck.

He couldn't stop drinking. It tasted so good. Each mouthful of liquid that slid down his throat lit a fire within and like a wild man he had to have his way and drink the woman dry.

When the blood was gone, he released his bite, stumbled back and fell to the ground. He lay there quivering, the aftermath of sheer euphoria taking him.

15

AFTER THROWING UP a lungful of river water, Marcus ran out from between the trees. "Shelly!" His steps immediately slowed upon seeing her. "Oh no. Shelly . . ."

He could barely stand. Despite all the blood he'd seen spilled in his lifetime, despite the nightmares, the fighting, the war, he wasn't prepared for this.

What was left of Shelly's body was still bound to the tree, her head hanging to one side. No weight was upon her feet. She just hung there limp, and he knew she was dead. He came up to his wife and raised a hand to touch her. It took a few moments before he could. Once he touched her, it would become final. He placed his hand on her cheek; her skin was cool, dry, not even a hint of moisture. His eyes travelled over her body and he saw the wound, a deep gash in her neck as wide and long as a vampire's mouth. Tears filled his vision and all he wanted to do was scream. He even tried, not caring if any undead haunting the forest heard him. All that came out was a raspy call, thick with anguish and tears.

Heart aching, he took his knife and cut Shelly free from her bonds. She collapsed into his arms. Marcus slowly lowered themselves to the ground and held her in his lap.

Shaking, he let the pain take him and put his face against hers. Tears poured over her lifeless body.

"You can't be dead," he said. "You can't. We're a team. I love you. You're my wife. Please, don't go."

Though he and Shelly had both prepared for and

talked about this day, each prayed it would never come.

It was over. His life was over. Without Shelly, there was nothing. Nothing except . . . Rose. The poor girl lost her mother tonight. No child should, especially to murder.

But what if she turns? Marcus thought. Even in the poor lighting, it was clear Shelly's skin was void of color. The skin was pale yellow, the blood having ceased pumping through it for some time now.

Marcus knew the final step, knew that even though it seemed his wife was dead, he had to make sure it would remain that way. The change varied from person to person. Sometimes it was mere minutes. Other times it took several months. Time was of the essence.

"I'm so sorry, sweetie," he said, laying her head on the ground. He could barely straighten himself to carry out the task at hand.

As gently as he could, he put the tip of the knife to his wife's chest, holding it upright above her skin.

"May God have mercy on the lives we led. May you find peace in His presence, and may He also explain to you why He let these creatures of Hell take the lives of so many, especially yours."

Tears blurring his vision, he raised the knife . . . and brought it down.

16

ROSE WASN'T FAR from home, and good thing, too. She was getting cold and her legs were sore from walking.

But it did you good, the walk, she thought. *Got some of the frustration out. Took your mind off things. Fresh air does wonders and all that. Going to rub it into Parker whenever I see him.*

She turned a corner and headed down her street, looking forward to getting into bed for a good night's sleep.

♦ ♦ ♦

Zach and his mother stood on top of the Richardson Building, looking out over the city. The streetlights below created a golden grid dotted with the white and red lights of cars.

"I'm proud of you, son," Mira said. "How do you feel?"

He heard his mother's voice, but was too lost in the sights below to offer a reply.

"Zach?"

He turned to her. "Changed. Complete. It's like before I was on the ledge of this building, learning what I am and who we are. Once I fed, it's like I dove off the ledge and plunged down to the city below to be among the people, really be encompassed by them."

She nodded.

"Do you understand?"

"I do. A vampire's first feed is the final step in their

transformation. Though you still have much to learn about your heritage, you are now truly one of us. There's no going back."

"I don't want to. I don't remember what it was like, so I'm not missing anything, and based on what you've taught me, why would I want to be something less than I am now?"

She smiled. "When you drank, what did you feel?"

"Pure pleasure, Mother. My whole body shook with it."

"Good."

"I felt my strength grow. I feel like I can do anything."

"You can."

"My thoughts are so clear, no longer fuzzy images and muted voices. I can see everything I want and need so clearly now."

"As it should be."

"And—" Zach dropped to his knees as his equilibrium disappeared. Darkness covered his vision and he sensed the transition of the images in his mind actually appearing before him.

He saw the woman on the tree, bound and blindfolded. A bright white flash snatched the image away, fading into the same woman walking the streets of Winnipeg in her long coat, moving through the forest by the river. Another bright flash and the woman was in an armory of some kind, gathering weapons and dressing herself. Another flash and the woman kissed a man.

There was a white flash between each image, Zach following the woman back through moments of her life before her death. The woman was kissing a man in a kitchen, in a bed. She walked the hallway of a house that Zach thought was familiar. A darkened room and a young girl lying in bed, her head turned away from the door. Putting in a sign outside a house reading SOLD; arguing in a kitchen with a beautiful young woman that reminded Zach of flowers; the same three people sitting around a dinner table, eating. Another flash and they were around the dinner table again, but someone else was with them.

A violent tingle swept through Zach's body when he recognized the other person: it was himself.

♦ ♦ ♦

Rose entered her house, flicked on the light in the landing, took off her shoes and went to the kitchen.

"Hello?" she called into the dark house.

No reply.

She checked the kitchen table and saw her note, and immediately recognized her father's handwriting beneath her own.

Had to run back to the office. Should be back soon.

Sorry.

Dad

"Well, whatever," she said, used to her parents' haphazard schedule. *What about Mom? And it's really late, too.*

It felt good to be back home.

Just going to head upstairs, put on pajamas and crash. The bath will have to wait, she thought.

It was only when she entered her room and saw the Heart Box that she thought about Zach again. For a short while there, she hadn't, and felt all the better for it.

With a sigh, she put the box in a nook under her night table and changed into her pajamas. She hit the bathroom to give her hair and teeth a brush, then went back to her room and crawled under the covers.

"What a sucky night," she said. "Just one thing after another."

She hoped her parents would be back soon. She didn't want to be alone in the house too much longer. Just knowing her folks were sleeping in the next room was enough to provide the security she needed right now and help her have a good night's rest.

They better get here soon, she thought, rolled onto her side, and closed her eyes. *Don't want to wake up and see they're still gone.*

17

Tʜᴇ ᴘʜᴏɴᴇ ʙᴇsɪᴅᴇ Rose's bed rang a little after 2 A.M. She let it ring several times, hoping one of her parents would get it. If not, after eight rings it would go to the answering machine. After the eighth ring, the phone went silent only to resume ringing again a few seconds afterward.

"Would somebody get that?" she shouted, hoping her folks would hear her.

On the sixth ring, she yelled, "Never mind," and picked it up for herself. "Hello?"

"Rose, it's Dad," her father said on the other end.

"Dad?" She looked at the clock. "It's 2:12. Where are you?"

"I'm out."

"Where's Mom?"

"She's with me. We're together. Get a pen and write this down."

"Write what down?"

"Just do it, okay? Really need your cooperation on this."

Rose turned on the lamp by her bed, winced at its bright glow, and pulled a pad of paper and a pen from her night table drawer. "Okay, what?"

He gave her an address to jot down and said to take the Saturn and go to the address on the paper.

"Who's house is this?" she asked. "Are you guys okay?"

Her father was slow to respond. "Just do as I say.

Make sure no one follows you either, okay?"

"Why would anyone—Seriously, Dad, what's going on? Are you both drunk and need a ride?"

"In a way," he said. "Just come here and don't let anybody see you."

"O-okay," she said.

"And, Rose?" His voice was thick with tears.

"Yeah?"

"I love you."

♦ ♦ ♦

Marcus beeped off his cell phone and stuck it back in his pocket. If he could, he would have gone and picked up Rose himself, but he couldn't leave Shelly. If any of the vampires followed him here without his knowledge, he could only imagine what they would do to the place never mind his wife's body.

Shelly was on a table near the wall of swords, covered with a blanket. Once Marcus had got her into the house via the garage, he immediately went to work examining her. More times than not he had to stop so he could let out the tears before working again. Right now, he still wanted to cry but nothing would come from his eyes. All he had was a splitting headache and sore, red skin around his eye sockets.

"Rose'll be here soon, hon," he said, a hand on his wife's body. "She's going to have to learn everything tonight despite us deciding we'd hold off." He knelt down beside the table and pulled back the blanket to expose his wife's face. Even like this, she was beautiful, and seemed to be at rest. "I'm so sorry for letting you down, sweetheart. I'm sorry for failing you." He glanced away and closed his eyes. Shelly was dead because of him.

He wanted to rescue her, but he couldn't. He should have fought harder. Should have simply attacked the vampires the moment he saw them. Shouldn't have let that one dunk him in the river.

He glanced back at his wife. When he spoke, sheer determination and solemn will coated his voice. "I swear, I will never let anything like this happen again. I swear on my own life Rose will be protected. I will watch over her day and night. As for the undead, I will show no mercy. I will kill every single one of them myself if it comes to it. They will pay for what they did to you and what they stole from Rose and I. You will be avenged."

Marcus put his forehead against hers, then gave her a kiss on the lips. "I love you, Shelly. Forever."

◆ ◆ ◆

It was almost three quarters of an hour before Rose arrived at the house on Valor Road. She pulled into the driveway, put the car in park, and looked at the house. All the lights were off.

Is this the right place? She checked the piece of paper where she'd written the address her dad had given her. What was written matched what was on the house.

She turned off the ignition, yawned, then got out of the car. "This better be good," she muttered.

Rose approached the front door, and rang the doorbell. After a few moments, footsteps arose within. She couldn't see the person on the other side due to the frosted window alongside the door. They didn't even bother to turn the light on, but instead just opened the door. It was her dad.

"Hey, honey," he said softly.

Between the shadows on his face, Rose noticed her

dad's bloodshot eyes. "What's wrong? What happened? Whose house is this?"

"Come inside."

She did and her father took her in his arms and held her tight. He was shaking, sobbing.

"What happened? Are you okay? Is Mom okay?" Rose asked, peering over his shoulder and finding the house empty.

Her father pulled away. He didn't have to say anything. His face said it all: her mother was dead.

Rose burst into tears and stood there with him in the front landing, her head on his shoulder. *How? Why? What happened?* "Were you . . . were you with her?"

Her dad sniffled. "No."

"Where . . . where is she?"

He didn't reply.

She shook as she cried. "Dad, where's Mom?"

Finally, he said, "Downstairs."

Rose's heart sank. Did her dad come to this house and find her? Did she slip and fall? Did she . . . kill herself? Where were the people that owned the place? Was she having an affair? Is that who killed her?

Her father gave her a loving squeeze, then said, "Come here, Rose. I want to show you something."

She pulled away and wiped the tears from her eyes. "What?"

He didn't say anything, but instead took her by the hand and led her through the dark house, past the kitchen, downstairs to a family room and then to a closed door. When he opened it, Rose saw there was a light on in the basement.

"I don't want to see this," she said.

"I know, but it'll be all right."

"How could it be all right if Mom's de—" She broke

down again, shoulders jerking with each painful sob.

"Here, let me help you." Her father put his arm around her shoulder and guided her down the basement steps. When they got to the bottom, they didn't go further into the room.

Rose couldn't believe what she saw: a cement-walled fortress, each wall lined with swords, knives, tools. A stand in the middle of the room held black one-piece outfits that looked to be made of plastic or metal. By the wall on the side was a table with something on it, a blanket draped over top. She squinted her eyes and knew the blanket was covering a body.

"What is this?" she asked.

"I don't know where to begin."

"Where's Mom? Is that her?" She pointed to the table, then took a step toward it.

"Yes."

Suddenly, a sharp thought hit her and a swell of anger bubbled within. She stepped even farther away from her father. "What, are you some kind of pyscho? Did you kill her?"

"Rose!" he shouted. Then his face went soft. His voice was gentle when he spoke again. "Of course not. I would never harm your mother. I know that by looking around this room, that could be what you're thinking. Please know I had nothing to do with what happened."

"Nothing?"

He glanced to the floor. "Not . . . nothing." He met her eyes. "But I didn't k-kill her."

"Dad, I swear, if you so much as laid a finger on her, I'll—" She didn't know what she'd do. Call the cops, that's for sure. She pulled her cell phone out of her pocket.

"What are you doing?"

"What does it look like I'm doing?" She began dialing 9-1-1, but only managed the first two digits before her father snatched the phone out of her hand. The way he moved was like lightning.

"You can't."

"Give me that!" She reached over and he shoved her arm away.

"Listen to me!" he snapped.

The sound of his voice made her jump.

Softly, he said, "Please listen to me." He pinched the bridge of his nose. "Your mother and I love you very much, Rose. We'd do anything for you. In fact, it's because of you that we have this house."

"This is—"

"Let me finish."

"Oh, Dad . . ." she breathed.

"This house is ours. We kept it a secret from you for your own protection until you were old enough. Then we were going to tell you what this is."

Was he crazy? Were her parents lunatics? Worse . . . murderers?

He beeped her cell phone off and put it in his own pocket. "Your mother and I," he said, "we . . . how should I say this?" He sighed. "We kill vampires."

She arched an eyebrow. *You're crazy.*

"We have since before you were born. My father did it. So did his father. So did even his father. We are called 'slayers,' in that we slay vampires. I know I sound crazy, but just hear me out. They're real and not just the things of stories. We did it to not only help other people, but also to try and make this city a safer place for you. All those late nights, those meetings with 'clients,' the times your mother and I had to run out of the house at a moment's notice—it was all because of this."

Rose's mind was blank. She didn't know what to think. How was she supposed to react to this? Her mom . . . . She glanced at the table by the wall of swords again.

"Your mother died tonight because she was out there doing what she thought was right. In a way, she died protecting you, even protecting me. I swear to you I'm telling the truth. I've never lied to you. The only thing I've kept secret is what your mother and I did when we weren't working. Honest. We needed to wait until you were older, until you were mature enough to process all this."

Rose took a deep breath. "I . . . I don't know what to say. I'm having a hard time believing you."

"I know."

"You sound like you're drunk and are trying to hide what really happened tonight."

"I know."

"Mom would never go along with whatever it is you're saying. Mom hated even killing a spider never mind some fake monster."

"I know."

"Will you quit it? I'm trying to talk here."

"I'm sorry."

"You should be, Dad." She needed to get out of here so she moved for the stairs.

He blocked her path. "Where are you going?"

"Away."

"You can't."

"Don't even try and keep me here."

"I don't want to, but I will. You have to understand this is a delicate matter."

"You think?"

"What I mean is your mother and I planned for this

day. We had hoped to tell you together, and we even talked about it earlier this afternoon, but your mom wanted to hold off a bit until you were over Zach."

The mere mention of his name pierced her heart. "Don't go there with me."

"I'm sorry. All I meant was we had wanted to tell you together, but we also talked about what we'd do if we couldn't. The only thing we could come up with was when one of us passed due to this . . . job . . . we'd tell you right away, bring you here and let you come to terms with things."

"You lie."

"Come on, Rose, look around. Do you think I'm lying? Okay, sure, maybe you think I'm lying about the vampire part, but in terms of your mother and I being mercenaries, what do you think? Who else keeps a basement like this?"

"I don't know, pyschos? Serial killers?"

"If you don't believe me about the vampire part, fine. We'll tackle that issue another time. But I'm telling you the truth."

She shook her head. "Just let me go, Dad."

"No."

Without thinking, she shoved him in the chest, pushing him back a step. The moment her foot touched down on the first stair, her dad grabbed her from behind and pulled her deeper into the room.

"Stop! Let go of me!" she screamed.

He took her past the table, around a corner, and to a door that had a pair of chains across it in an X. With one hand, he clutched her close to his body; with the other he fished a key off a ring on his belt. He slid the key into the padlock keeping the chains together and unlocked it.

"Dad! Stop!" she shouted.

"Quiet. I'm giving you proof."

The padlock came loose and the chains draped to the side like a pair of curtains. He then punched a code into the keypad above the door handle and a loud *ka-thoom* shook Rose's insides. Her father opened the door with a grunt and set her down inside. He threw on the lights.

"Look around," he said.

The room was as big as a wine cellar, narrow, with what looked like silver coffins stacked three high and two deep on either side. There was another stack of two next to the wall across from them.

"What is this?" she asked.

"This is where we keep them, if they don't disintegrate upon death. There are vampires in these coffins. We keep them contained here in case, through some miracle, they come back to life after we thought we disposed of them. In the old days, you could chop off their head and would be assured they would not regenerate. Seems some have increased in power as those contained here regenerated their heads after being decapitated." He pulled a sword off the wall next to the door and proceeded to the first coffin.

"What are you doing?" she asked.

"Come here and watch."

"I don't . . . I don't want to."

"Fine, then stay there but don't leave this room. You want proof that I'm not crazy? That I'm telling the truth? Fine. This is it." He turned a switch that looked like a large butterfly nut on the side of the coffin. Another *ka-thoom* shook the room, then the lid on the coffin slid to the side, retreating inside the wall away from her father.

Her dad pointed the sword against what was within.

"No sudden movements," he said, "but you can look."

Rose glanced to the door. She couldn't believe what was going on.

"Rose?" her dad said.

With a sigh, she went over beside him and looked in the coffin. Her breath caught in her throat when she saw the body within. She couldn't tell if it was male or female, but it lay there like a decomposing corpse, the skeleton beneath pushing up against its drooping skin. Its dark clothing was in tatters, a large silver spike of some kind protruding from its chest, roughly where its heart would be. The tip of her father's sword was against where the spike met the flesh in a cakey mess of dried blood and rotten meat.

The skull was without eyes, only the sockets remaining, its hooded brow sharp and pronounced. Its mouth open, large sharp teeth lining it.

Rose put a hand to her mouth and also pressed the side of her index finger and thumb against her nose the smell was so bad.

"See?" her dad said. "I was telling the truth."

18

ZACH WAS IN the crypt with his family. He sat alone, his back against his coffin, knees up, elbows upon them.

Mira had explained that what he saw were flashes from the woman's life, prominent memories that she'd held dear.

It was the image of himself he saw in the montage that bothered him the most. He didn't tell Mira that part, not really sure how to even bring it up.

"Those of whom we drink blood become a part of us in that way," she had told him. "The secrets and memories that were revealed to you are now your own. It is how we gain wisdom and learn to utilize it to ensure our survival."

Zach wasn't completely sure his not mentioning the image of himself was a complete secret anyway. These people could read his mind and he'd thought about what he saw several times since returning to the crypt. He just wished he knew how to read his family's minds and how to block them from reading his own.

One thing at a time, he thought. He'd already learned so much, and apparently his father was to teach him even more tomorrow night.

The image of that woman, though. He felt a connection to her in a way he hadn't to anything else since he'd been reborn. The woman . . . he couldn't help but feel he'd seen her before, and not only her, but others in the images that flashed through his mind afterward as well. The man whom he presumed was the woman's husband, and the young lady who was as intriguing as she was beautiful. When he brought the image of the three of them to the fore of his mind, there was a warmth that permeated from the thought that swept through him, a sense of not only familiarity about them, but of belonging.

Were these people his family from time's past? Was he their son? Did he just kill his own mother? The human one?

He stood as Wil came up to him.

"So, how was it?" Wil asked.

"Unlike anything I've ever experienced before."

Wil smiled. "You've just been reborn and suffer memory loss. Everything is unlike anything you've ever experienced before."

Zach smirked. "I suppose, but I do have a question."

"Shoot."

"If you guys are my family, then who was I with before I came here?"

"Ah. You mean your Surrogates."

"Surrogates?" He didn't know the word.

"Yeah, surrogates. They're substitutes, if you will. I had some at one point, too, so did Cassie. Our mother and father gave us up for adoption when we were born. You see, if your parents were pure-blood vampires, you yourself would be born one, too. But if your parents aren't, meaning they didn't descend directly from the first vampires, then their offspring are born human despite their being undead."

"Huh?"

"Okay, to simplify: Mother and Father weren't always vampires. They were born human and were eventually bitten so turned into vampires. With me so far?"

"Yeah."

"As a result, the vampirism isn't the dominant thing in their genes so when they had kids, the dominant side usually is what was born, in our case, humans."

"So why not just turn the baby into a vampire and raise it as one?"

"Because the vampire gene is recessive, it has to mature before it can be—what's the word? Activated?—for turning. Usually around the time kids are in their teens. That's what Mother says, anyway."

"So other humans raised us until—"

"Until Mother came for us and brought us home."

It made sense, but was a hard thing to swallow. Not only was Zach meeting this strange new family, he was now being told he had another one out there as well.

"Have you . . . gone back to your other family?" he asked Wil.

"Once, but I didn't let them see me. Mother said it would be too upsetting and could cause problems for us."

"Like . . . ?"

"The family could have slayer connections and we could be found out pretty quick. It'd be really easy to put two and two together."

"What about changing your old family into vampires?"

"Father said that every time a slayer has been turned—assuming your old family were slayers—it always ends in bloodshed. *Our* blood. Turning a slayer, he said, was like a human angering one bee outside of its hive. It goes back in and gets an entire swarm of them to come after you. It's just too dangerous." Wil glanced back at Mira, Rain and Cassie, who were sitting around talking on Mira's coffin in the middle of the room. "I wouldn't want to die. Not again. The things I can do now, the life I lead, there are very few restrictions and I'm more powerful now than I ever was in my previous life."

"And if they weren't slayers?"

"Can't risk it."

Zach thought he was being too paranoid. He furrowed his brow. "Do you remember your previous life?"

"Now I do. It took a while but it eventually came to me. Different memories from different blood triggered my own memories until, eventually, everything became clear."

"And you don't miss them, your family?"

"No."

"Why not?"

"The change adjusted my outlook on everything, as I'm sure you've already noticed for yourself."

He was right. Ever since the beginning Zach had a fairly easy time believing what he was told and shown. Something within confirmed all that was revealed to him as fact and even as part of the life he now led. There was also this sense of *immersion* in the vampire world, as if he was just one drop in a pond, intermixed and mingled with all the other drops. He was one, and they were one, and he was one with them.

"I have so much to learn," Zach said almost in afterthought.

"Father will help you with that. He's the oldest of us and knows more than anyone of us combined."

"How long have you been a vampire?"

"Forty-two years."

Forty-two years? Zach thought. *He only looks twenty-something.*

"Mother turned me when I was twenty-one. Time stands still once you've been turned. For most of us, anyway. Sometimes the old life has trouble letting go and you continue to age for a short period before finally stopping."

"You mean I'll be this way . . . forever?"

"Pretty much."

Zach let the idea soak in. Yet a part of him also felt cheated out of a full life despite what he got in return. He had barely begun living before becoming one of them, was only human for a short time. It would have been nice to live a longer life even if that meant being a lesser being for a larger period of time. And after the images he saw once drinking that woman's blood, being human didn't seem too bad either.

19

Over the next few days, Rose divided her time between the home she grew up in and the home her parents had used for their nocturnal activities. Her father had taken time off work, even so far as passing any home deals in the works onto others he knew in the business.

"Family comes first," he said.

Rose was given time off school to grieve, which she did plenty of. Yesterday afternoon was spent in her room, crying into her pillow for at least an hour straight before getting herself together enough to take a shower.

As for her mother's funeral, her father informed her that due to her unique death, slayers had procedures in place for such an occurrence, their people stationed in various city jobs to handle the required paperwork for a slayer's passing. Certain reports had to be forged and signed off on. Insurance policies needed to come into play, questions needed to be answered. Rose was amazed at the operation, but if everything her father had been telling her over the last few days was true, then her mother's memory would be safe, both on paper and in the hearts of those she knew.

The funeral was coming up in three days and preparations were already underway in terms of internment for the body.

"You have a crypt for vampires," Rose had told her dad, "but not for you guys?"

"The crypt for the undead, as mentioned, is for those who don't disintegrate at death. It's more of a vault than a crypt, actually. As for us slayers, we've lived our whole lives as normal as possible on the surface. We also die as normal as possible, so the eyes of the world see that, like them, we return to dust. But there is a place overseas where the memory of slayers is preserved and a plaque will be mounted in your mother's honor for her years of service. You and I will go there one day, when you're ready."

"I'm ready now," she said. "How about after the funeral?"

"I would love to," he said, "but the funeral is but the beginning for you, for you shall follow in your mother's footsteps and train to take her place."

Rose sighed. "Dad, I've been really patient with you. I've listened to everything you've told me and, even after what you've shown me, I'm still coming to terms with it all. A part of me believes you, another part is waiting to wake up and get on with life. But if indeed this is reality, then I don't want to be a part of this. Even just being part of it now for Mom's sake is hard enough. I'm hoping that once everything settles, you and I can just move on and forget any of this ever happened."

"I appreciate the sentiment, I really do, but we can't."

"Why? 'They' won't let you?"

"No. But I know that which I fight, and it's something I cannot walk away from. As for you, yes, you do have a choice, but I want you to carefully consider it. Don't let grief over your mother interfere with your decision."

"How can you be so cold like that? You sound like Mom's death was all in the line of duty or something, and once she's laid to rest, that's it and life goes on with you heading down the same path that killed her."

"I don't expect you to understand."

"You're right . . . I *don't* understand."

"One day you will."

"I don't want to."

"You will."

Rose rolled her eyes and stormed out of the room.

◆ ◆ ◆

On the day of Shelly Jordan's funeral, the sky was overcast and there was a slight chill on the air. The limousine rolled up to Eagle Park Cemetery just past eleven o'clock in the morning. Rose stepped out of the limo and her father came out behind her. Other members of Shelly's family, Rose's cousins, and others on her dad's side drove up in their own vehicles, everyone somber, eyes cast down to the ground.

The priest led the way through the cemetery, leading the family to the shelf-like crypt—a columbarium—where Shelly's ashes would be laid to rest. Marcus wanted it that way, and Rose knew most of the reasons had to do with his other "job."

"We can't preserve the body," her father had told her. "Your mother and I already talked about this. We must purge any chance of infection with fire, even if the other was killed rather than turned. Likewise, by cremating the remains, they become useless to any vampire who might learn our true identities and use the body as leverage against us at a later date."

Rose understood, but that didn't mean she liked it. "Your life is governed by slaying the undead, isn't it?"

Her father looked her in the eye. "Yes, but so was your mother's, and please don't view it as a hindrance. It is not. It is an honor."

Now, after the funeral service in the church, Rose and

her father stood before the vertical crypt, the door to her mother's cubbie in the columbarium open. Her father held the urn containing her mother's ashes, the urn itself inside a black velvet bag.

"If you would, please, Mr. Jordan," Father Melnick said.

Rose's father nodded, brought the velvet bag close to his chest, and gave it a squeeze. "Rose," he said, and the two walked together to lay Shelly in her eternal resting place. "Together."

Rose cupped her hands under her father's, and together they brought the bag with the urn to the open columbarium and set the bag within.

Tears in her eyes, she whispered, "Bye, Mom. I love you. I'll do my best to take care of Dad."

She turned away, only to hear her father whisper to his wife, "Until we meet again. I love you, Shelly."

They returned to their place before the columbarium, while the priest finished the eulogy.

Family and friends gathered around the Jordans, sobbing, some putting hands on each other's backs. A few embraced in sorrowful hugs.

Marcus Jordan held his daughter tight, and Rose held him even tighter. Her world had changed, she knew. Not only had she lost her mother, but she had also lost her father, the man she knew before learning he was a slayer.

Zo

ZACH SAT OUTSIDE his family's mausoleum, his back against its side. Despite it being daylight, the overcast clouds kept the majority of the sun's rays from his skin. Rain, had told him that while direct sunlight was fatal, cloudy weather was not. However, UV rays still filtered through the clouds and, out here, Zach felt them on his exposed hands and face. His skin was hot, a subtle burn, but right now the heat was a distraction from his thoughts.

In the past few days, he had hunted each night, once each with Rain, Wil and Cassie. The thrill of snatching prey from the streets of the city was almost as exciting as the moment before he bit into his victim's neck and bled them dry, their blood a launchpad into a tidal wave of euphoria. The aftermath of his victims' memories was something he also looked forward to, as each image flashing before his eyes connected him further with his old life and how things were before he was reborn.

Last night, he had found a street walker by an old warehouse on Higgins, tugged her into the shadows and breathed in her perfume before parting her red hair and feasting on her blood. After, sitting on the ground beside her body, rocking from the pleasure, Wil standing guard, he saw the woman as a little girl. Saw her father beat her. Saw stacks of homework as the woman tried to make something of herself. He learned she had been a medical student, but had to drop out early because she didn't have enough money to finish her schooling. Worse, she was only a year away. After some odd jobs, she fell into habitual drug use, and soon worked the street as a means to survive and support her habit.

It was the images of school that rocked Zach's world and reminded him of his own wandering the halls, heading to class, opening and closing his locker. During one of the flashbacks, his locker door closed and a beautiful girl stood on the other side. She had long brown hair that sat in ringlets on her shoulders, her bright hazel eyes sparkling despite the poor hallway lighting. Her lips were pink and plush, the kind that made him ache to touch them with his fingertips.

It was the same girl in the flashback where he saw himself around a dinner table.

The connection was there, taunting him from within. Obviously, he knew her, but whether she was someone he kind of knew, was related to or something else, that he wasn't sure. Yet there was something else about her, something that told him she had meant a great deal to him.

As he sat outside the mausoleum, he wondered if the tugging on his heart was real, or if it was a phantom sensation from his old life.

Rain had told him that as memories were slowly restored, some days would be easier than others. Some days were to be filled with questions, while others would be filled with answers and moments of reflection.

"Just wish I knew who she was," Zach said. He rubbed his hands on the damp grass that was still wet from the rain from the night before. The cool water helped sooth the heat upon his skin.

He stood and floated a few inches above the ground, the sense of leaving gravity behind helping lift the weariness inside. He needed to get back inside the crypt soon, not only to sleep but to get out from under the clouds and heal.

It wasn't long before he noticed he had floated far from where he should be. He was under strict orders not to wander far from his family's crypt. He still had so much to learn, his mother told him, and she didn't want to risk anything going wrong while he was without supervision.

Behind the next row of tombstones, there was a gathering of people. Zach touched down and walked silently on the grass, keeping himself in line with the trees so he wouldn't be seen.

This was the first time he saw such a crowd in the cemetery since waking here. When he did see someone, it was usually just one or two people at a time to visit the grave of a loved one.

Zach went behind a tree around thirty feet from the gathering and looked on. Some of the people were crying. Others merely stood there with blank expressions. A few were huddled together in an embrace. Were they all here to visit someone now deceased? There were about thirty people in all, ranging in age from around ten to over seventy.

Zach listened intently, and the man in the black shirt and pants beyond saying, ". . . Father, Son and Holy Ghost. May Your servant, O God, rest in peace. Ashes to ashes, dust to dust. Amen."

The man in black moved out of the way, revealing two figures at the fore of everyone else.

They were the same people from the flashback after his first feeding. The man, tired and worn—and the girl, beautiful and mystifying.

♦ ♦ ♦

Rose's father closed the door to the columbarium, and locked it. It would be sealed up later with a plaque put in place with her mother's name, date of birth and date of death, and a note of sentiment.

Marcus put a hand around her shoulder and gave it a squeeze. "It's going to be okay."

The tears fell anew and Rose put her face in her hands. Her dad brought her in to a full hug and rubbed her back.

"It's okay," he said, "let it all out."

Rose's eyes glanced over the columbarium. She could envision her mother's ashes in there, the same ashes that once composed her actual body. Her mom. Already she missed her mother's smile, her laugh, the occasional nights she tucked Rose in despite her being a teenager.

A sharp pain running through her heart in waves, she told her dad she wanted to say good-bye to her mother one last time, alone.

"Sure, go ahead," he said softly.

Rose went up to the columbarium and laid her fingers on it. "Mom . . ." she said, but was cut short when she saw the face of a young man looking at them from behind a tree not too far away.

A thunderclap slammed through her heart and her mouth went dry. *No . . .* "It can't be . . ."

The young man pulled away in behind the tree.

"Zach?" she whispered.

Her father came up behind her and put a hand on her shoulder. "Rose?"

"Dad, I saw—" She glanced back toward the tree and she thought she saw someone running past the tombstones beyond, the person's motion so fluid it looked like they were gliding across the grass instead of running on it.

"Honey?" her dad said.

"I have to—" And before she realized it, her legs were already moving under her. *I can't believe this. Is it him? Can't be. What would he be doing here?* She ran around a row of tombstones, past a few trees, her father calling her name somewhere behind her.

She tripped over a stray tree branch and fell, her hands blocking her fall before her face hit the grass. She lay there a moment, catching her breath, elation and hurt pulling her feelings to either side.

Broken and tired, she slowly got to her feet. Palms stinging, she checked them over for scratches. They were only grass-stained; she gently brushed them together and dusted off the blades that stuck to her skin.

The cemetery around her was empty aside from her party, just a sea of tombstones and trees.

"I'm losing it," she said. "I thought I saw—" Someone was behind her. Rose spun around and a wave of dizziness passed through her when Zach stood before her.

Her legs gave out; he swiftly caught her before she hit the ground.

"Zach?" she said, scrambling to get her own two legs under her. *No, it's impossible!* "You're . . . you're . . ."

"How do you know my name?" he asked.

"How do I—Zach, it's me, Rose. Remember? We're dat—"

Mr. Jordan called out to her a few rows away.

"I can't stay," Zach said.

"What? Why? Where have you been? I've been worried sick. Oh, Zach." She ran up to hold him and fell into his arms.

"Who are you?" he asked.

She didn't answer, but instead shut her eyes and squeezed him tight.

"Rose!" It was her father.

Right before she opened her eyes, her arms passed through the air and she was clasping herself.

Her father grabbed her and shook her. "Rose! Are you okay? Did it—did he—"

"Dad," she said. "It was Zach. He's alive."

From beyond the tombstones, Mira looked on. *Come home, Zach dear. Do not worry about them now.*

Contact had been made.

Everything was going to plan.

About the Author

A.P. Fuchs is the author of many novels and short stories, most of which have been published. His most recent books are *Possession of the Dead, Magic Man Plus 15 Tales of Terror* and *Zombie Fight Night: Battles of the Dead*, in which zombies fight such classic monsters as werewolves, vampires, Bigfoot, and even go up against awesome foes like pirates, ninjas, and . . . Bruce Lee.

A.P. Fuchs is also known for his superhero series, *The Axiom-man Saga*, and the author of the shoot 'em up zombie trilogy, *Undead World*. He also edited the zombie anthologies *Dead Science* and *Vicious Verses and Reanimated Rhymes: Zany Zombie Poetry for the Undead Head*.

Fuchs lives and writes in Winnipeg, Manitoba.

Visit his corner of the Web at
www.canisterx.com

Check out the *Undead World Trilogy* at
www.undeadworldtrilogy.com

And follow him on Twitter at
www.twitter.com/ap_fuchs

Did you know **A.P. Fuchs** writes love stories under the pen name **Peter Fox**?

For touching love stories that tug at the heartstrings, look no further than the following:

When a quirky girl named April suddenly sits across from Joseph Bailey at a quiet coffee shop, nothing can prepare him for the weekend ahead and how it'll change him forever.

Jack used to believe in angels.

Her name was Cyan, and they were in love.

Peter Fox books are available in paperback and eBook at Amazon.com or your favorite online retailer.

A.P. Fuchs
Zombie Collection

Axiom-man
The Dead Land
ISBN 978-1-897217-83-2

Blood of the Dead
ISBN 978-1-897217-80-1

Possession of the Dead
ISBN 978-1-926712-53-6

Vicious Verses and
Reanimated Rhymes
ISBN 978-1-897217-95-5

Available at Amazon.com, BarnesandNoble.com
or your favorite online retailer.

Also available through your favorite bookstore.

www.coscomentertainment.com